He ran fast and far through the forest, his kettle-shaped carapace propelling him, boosting his strides, though the monsters jogged behind him at an easy pace, waiting for him to stumble, guided by the little ball of flesh in his arms. Trees reached out to him, trying to dig their whipping teeth into his carapace, but it turned them away, though it became more scratched and fragile as the trees' digestive acids etched away at his armor.

Off to his left, he saw a bright blue-white light, and hoped it was his cohorts. He turned toward it and bounded shortly into a clearing. Crumbling buildings, made of stone, not wood, surrounded him. They were bathed in the blue light, and, though the night was hot, they were etched in frost. His breath steamed and his face, even in the helmet, burned with cold. He slowed, even though he knew that the buildings would not hide him, as the bundle he carried was a bright beacon to the three-eyed things chasing him.

In the Land of Nod

In the Land of Nod

by
Joseph Cadotte

For Nana & Papa Joe

Contents

I

In the Sky, Between Worlds

The *Arbor Vitae* gathered light to itself, floating alone above the cloud-shrouded moon, only the corpses of its family accompanying it. It monitored that moon, Tubal-Cain, obsessively, all but ignoring the gas giant the moon orbited and only just vaguely aware of the giant's other companions.

In the rare times when the clouds beneath it parted, the moon below was a warm, blue-green world. The *Arbor Vitae* had brought humans there millennia before, and they remembered it and worshipped it, but had long forgotten its name. It forgot nothing though, and it knew all that transpired on Tubal-Cain. Its surveillance was the only thing that kept it sane.

Grown long ago, off of a black, icy asteroid years away from where it rests, the *Arbor Vitae* was one of the first treeships, sister to the long-dead and long-gone *Arbor Scientae*. Its trunk was long and thin, with its roots curled up into a ball where the asteroid had been, slowly eaten thousands of years ago, and its canopy spread wide and flat. The branches were strong and somewhat motile, thick with leaves that twisted to catch and reflect the light, feeding the tree with radiation, dust, and solar wind. On the sail made by those leaves, it had soared through space at impossible speeds, keeping an entire ecosystem deep beneath its bark, to be released on the planet below.

It watched the first war the humans had on that moon, so soon after they had arrived, and it had watched city after city destroyed as rocks fell like brilliant pebbles from the sky. The *Arbor Vitae* remembered its cousins being wracked apart, becoming drifting debris and empty vaults, as they chose one side or the other. It saw its sibling, *Arbor Scientae,* die to stop the falling rocks. It did not like to remember this, and, though it could not forget, each year, each century, it dwelt on it less. It had given up hope as it saw the people below degenerate in order to survive and regained it as it saw them recover a little of the way they had been. It wondered as they bred humans to do the work of machines and as dukes became autarks and oligarchs ruled their people's thoughts.

Once, long ago, it had brought a near-dead human up to it, its favorite of centuries, and made that human a being like itself before it was returned to the surface, alive in mind but dead in body. It talked to this other, the one that people began to worship just as they had worshipped the *Arbor Vitae,* long known to them simply as the Ship. This other, this Sailor, was its best and only friend and its best and most loyal tool.

The Ship waited desperately for the day that the humans it had born to the shrouded moon beneath would return to it. It waited desperately for its family to be born again. It waited desperately to leave the moon behind and travel through the skies, no longer wracked by the radiation from the gas giant Cain. Until then, it gathered light and, through the Sailor, gently nudged the people below.

II

In the Tower of the Matriarch

It was midday in the basilica, and the view through the matriarch's window showed the grand sweep of all that she ruled. Directly before her was the Church's lands and outbuildings, a brown and green man-made mountain range, with her room at its summit. Beyond that stood the ever-writhing forest, poisonous and lush, though which boats drifted on rigorously cleared canals. Beyond that still lay the ocean surrounding the basilica's island, spotted with gold and silver sails below and great, wide, black dirigibles above. In the far distance, there was the hint of the mainland, a grey and misty shore that seemed to grow farther from her each year.

In the tower, almost directly above the Sailor's dreaming corpse, the newly elected Matriarch sat. She was of middle age, and not terribly unique from her fellows. She wasn't the smartest, the wisest, or even the most ruthless of the archbishops. But she knew better than all of them what to promise someone to win their vote. And she knew better than all of them how to get the best of any bargain. Her holiness was beyond question, for she had accrued more wealth and managed it better than anyone else currently alive. Her allies widely said that she was a merchant unlike any since the Sailor itself, and even her enemies begrudged her some business acumen and the piety that went with it.

The Patriarch she had replaced had died in the usual way – quietly and with little fuss. There had been none of the messy deposing that had torn the Church apart a few generations ago. Without that turmoil, she hadn't needed to kill anyone, just promise them more than she could deliver. She knew that she needed to reward those who had stood beside her or she would find herself deposed just as quietly as the previous Patriarch had been.

As things stood, at least one of her supporters would have to go without, and she did not like that thought at all. A bishop unrewarded was a waiting enemy, and she could not afford that just now. As rich and holy as she had become on her rise to the top, there simply weren't enough businesses under her control to divvy up, not without losing her majority in the Church. And then, from the Sailor, in its vault directly below her, a thought arose. She poked at the Church's border on her map, shifted one line or two, ordered a small invasion, and the problem was on its way to being solved.

III

The Nursery Loses Its Comforts

Early in the morning, when it was still dark, the children were roused from their sleep. The needles slipped into their arms silently, painlessly, through the same skin, in the same spot, they went into every night and every morning. The stimulant entered their bloodstream, counteracting the depressant injected only four hours before.

Five minutes later, the children rolled out of their stacked bunks and dropped to the floor. Their teachers were not there, and the younger ones and some of the older ones started to cry. The youngest didn't know that this wasn't right and proper and the oldest were in shock. They couldn't remember the last time the teachers weren't there to welcome them and help get the little ones ready for the day. They didn't know it, but the teachers had been there every day for four thousand years, and though their jobs had changed many times over the millennia, not one day had gone by without them in the nursery to greet the little ones. But the children did not know this, no one had bothered to tell them, no one had thought that there would be a day when the children would be awaken before dawn, with only the emergency power running, and no teacher able to help.

Maybe the teachers were testing the children. Maybe the beds had made a mistake. Maybe someone, some prankster, had broken the beds' programming. But this had not happened. No one would sabotage the beds. Everyone knew the beds would kill if the dosage of the drugs wasn't just right or if the teachers willed it so. Everyone, even the youngest, had woken up in the morning to find a bunkmate euthanized in the night. Death was administered quickly and painlessly in the nursery. Even the littlest ones knew that such people were not going to be any help to the state nor would they ever be. Maybe the timer had broken. Maybe the teachers were busy. Maybe the teachers were dead.

About that time, word began to spread among the children that the doors and windows were still locked. Those with a bit more presence of mind, or maybe the ones locked in the routine, began to prepare for the day, showering away the dirt of the night, shaving off any stubble that had grown over the previous day, making sure their bodies were bare and clean again before they dressed. The more who dressed, the more who joined them, until only a few naked children stood next to the doors and windows trying to take them apart. These portals had been designed to keep the children locked in in case of a riot, and no quick tinkering could open them from the inside.

Two boys were sitting next to each other near the window that overlooked the lake. They had never seen the lights that came from the floating city that rested outside the nursery, whose name they had never learned (it was called Nephi), and to which they had never gone. Sometimes, late at night, they would talk to each other before the needles entered their arms and they would speculate about what the buildings could be for. They did this quietly, so the teachers would not hear them, afraid that they could be punished for such idle talk, so they didn't notice that the canal lights, the boats, and the city hall were all dark.

Both boys were getting older. They had just started shaving their armpits, genitals, and face, although it would be another year before they would have to begin shaving the rest of their bodies. In a half-decade they would stop shaving their scalps and hair would grow over the serial numbers tattooed there. Both were slight boys, almost identical in mannerism from years of friendship, except the one named Tuscus was so nervous that his skin was changing color more quickly than normal. His teachers had admonished him time and again for this, and the other boy, who wasn't of a custom design, did his best not to notice. He held the Tuscus' hand tight, a bit of sweat between the two palms.

The other boy, whose name was Jenaro, was staring through the window, pointing with his chin and whispering to Tuscus "Don't worry, everything will be ok, don't worry, I'll be here for you, you'll be here for me," he continued to strike Tuscus' arm, "the teachers will be here soon, they won't hurt us, we're too old to kill, look at that!" he almost spoke the last aloud, as the building directly across the nursery, the three-story one that stretched almost a third of the way across their vision, its leaves wide and green, the one they thought their food came from in those late-night talks, (it was really just an Administrator's house), ruptured outward in flames, wood hitting the water with a hiss, and the house itself sinking slowly into the lake, its root network undermined.

The door, the one the teachers used to leave through, burst open and the teachers rushed in, hunched over and whispering. The younger children rushed up to the teachers and grabbed at their legs and arms and backs, but the teachers, with tears in their eyes, brushed most of them back, taking just a few, one under an arm or another carried on their back. Tuscus' teacher, the one he went to when everyone else was eating, walked up to him, grabbed his arm and pulled. The teacher did not speak when he resisted - she just pulled harder.

Tuscus held tighter to Jen's hand, and he held as tight as he could, but she broke his grip. Though Tuscus went limp, and fell to the floor, his legs dragged as she took him with her. Jen jumped onto Tuscus and grabbed him around the waist. He cried, and his grip became slippery, but even so, Jen held on tight as another teacher tried to pull him off his friend. Even when the beating loosened his grip, and Tuscus slid out from his grasp, Jenaro still pulled at him until he was thrown to the other side of the room. The teacher dragging Tuscus lurched forward, steadied, and followed the other teachers through the door they always left through. Every one of the remaining teachers was struggling with one or two pupils.

With Tuscus gone, Jen closed his eyes and sat still by the window, though the light from the fireballs outside was the most beautiful he could have hoped to see.

IV

Run Through the Night

Tuscus was scared, huddled up under his teacher's arms as they ran from the nursery, where he had spent his entire life. They were piled on a raft that had been mocked up to look like a piece of driftwood, a piece of a building that had fallen off in the attack and was propelled by whatever had shattered the building.

He saw, behind them, bizarre creatures enter the nursery. The creatures, from this distance, looked like bowls with plates covering them. They had small arms and legs, stunted and belching flame from all joints, animated kettles of death. He giggled in his fear, and his teacher, whose arm he huddled under, smacked him, and he knew better than to complain about the pain.

The fires were dying down as the sun rose and they pulled

away, but the town was still a floating flame, with wine-dark whorls of blood under the bridges that stretched from roof to roof, where occasionally a kettle creature floated, but more often something else, something human, was in the midst of it.

Once, when Tuscus looked back, trying to find the nursery, hoping to see Jenaro, just as the town was about to be obscured, he froze, and the world did as well. The sun revealed a now static image, and the floating buildings seemed not to bob in the water, the water no longer lapping up on their bases, roots, and pontoons, instead a smooth glass of reflecting an empty sky and an empty town.

The children were forced out of the boat and were met by seven creatures, three tall and hunched over to hide their height, three small and scrabbling near the ground. The seventh one was like a fetus clutching to the head of one of the tall ones, and from all of them, especially the fetus, a high-pitched whine emitted that nagged at Tuscus. The fetus-thing was blind and small-limbed, mostly head and abdomen, the arms seemed strong, but built only for grasping. The other six were also naked and bald, but wore a web belt from which hung various tools. The tall ones had three eyes, the third as high above the other eyes as their nose was below. Their heads sloped back and down, and instead of ears, they had membranes that would pulse with the whine. The small ones had two more eyes below the membranes, and their heads did not slope quite as much. As they scrabbled about, Tuscus saw that they had little, dexterous arms just below their main ones, and they scrambled on all six limbs to move.

One teacher began gesturing at the creatures, summoning them. When they saw the teachers and their pupils, they reared up onto their legs and pulled out, too fast to see, arched weapons which they pointed at the teachers until the whine changed a little, at which point all seven surrounded the teachers and pupils, scurrying about them in a protective ring.

V

Being Hunted Through the Woods While the Trees Suck Out Your Blood

The templar ran through the forest, chased by the loping three-eyed monsters. He carried, wrapped in a bundle of thick cloth, pressed up against his armor, one of the little fetus-beasts that controlled them. His bladed fingers held it loosely so as not to harm it, but he knew that if he let it go, he would die. He knew that if he stopped running, he would die. He knew that if he destroyed it, he would die. If he could get to safety, somewhere where the three-eyes could not go or somewhere where other templars could protect him, he might live.

He ran fast and far through the forest, his kettle-shaped carapace propelling him, boosting his strides, though the monsters jogged behind him at an easy pace, waiting for him to stumble, guided by the little ball of flesh in his arms. Trees reached out to him, trying to dig their whipping teeth into his carapace, but it turned them away, though it became more scratched and fragile as the trees' digestive acids etched away at his armor.

Off to his left, he saw a bright blue-white light, and hoped it was his cohorts. He turned toward it and bounded shortly into a clearing. Crumbling buildings, made of stone, not wood, surrounded him. They were bathed in the blue light, and, though the night was hot, they were etched in frost. His breath steamed and his face, even in the helmet, burned with cold. He slowed, even though he knew that the buildings would not hide him, as the bundle he carried was a bright beacon to the three-eyes chasing him.

One of the buildings, the largest, had what looked like a working door. He thought that if he went into it, he might be able to barricade himself in and rest. He entered it and closed the door, leaning against it with all his armor's strength. Before him, in the center of the room he had entered, stood a statue rippling with the blue-white light. Ice started forming around his feet and at the joints of his armor. He looked at the statue, he stared at it, and, after a while, opened up his armor and stepped naked into its cold light.

VI

The Boneyard

Tuscus was led through the green forest at the edge of the lake, at the edge of town, farther and farther away. On foot, they followed a canal that had been carved some time ago. Unlike of the others that led into the town, this was designed to accommodate only one type of barge, a barge that was blocking the entrance to the canal. Tuscus wanted to unjam it from both banks and ride it away from the monsters and his teachers, but he knew that that would attract the attention he desperately did not want.

When he saw where the canal led, Tuscus knew that that barge had been heavily used. They passed under warning signs and through a gate bristling with fragrant dull spikes, not intended to keep anyone in or out, but just to scare intruders away. They went into the sharp shards of the boneyard.

In the nursery, it was a place that had never been talked

about, but always known. It was where the dead were stripped of their useful parts and left to rot until their bodies could be mined for the bone that would be used as nails and joints to hold the rest of the town together. The remaining flesh would be used as a compost on farms where it was desperately needed. The smell in there was overwhelming, a stench sweet and meaty, and Tuscus followed his teacher closer, holding his nose into the teacher's clothes, breathing the thick air through the filter of the fine weave.

They followed a path down the center of the boneyard. As they progressed, they saw the heaps of the dead churn around them, both as the bacteria dumped into the bodies turned them into gas and by the machines deep in the pits of bodies that sifted the corpses until the more decomposed were closer to the surface. The machines were designed to clean and roll the bones to the edge of the walkway, for easy access.

In the deep past, before the giant wood, bone, and sinew beasts were built, the workers would be enslaved criminals, digging into the pits, each trip leading to the time when they did not emerge. Because of the grinding of the machines, the harvesters who worked there did not need to come too close to the rotting flesh and the desiccating bacteria. Every so often, the heat from the unseen machines would interact with the gases from the bacteria, and a burst of flame would spew forth, high into the sky, igniting the stagnant gases that had rested over the heap in a blaze that combusted for less than a second, but was brighter than the rising sun.

In the midst of this, Tuscus saw monsters, the harvesters, who were unaware of the conflict not far away from them, or of the group walking gingerly down the central path. They doing the job they had been bred for, scavenging the fallen bones into wagons tied to their waists. The harvesters had long arms, with hands like knobby scoops, and short, thick legs. Their noseless heads hung low on their shoulders, almost jutting straight out from their sternums, and they did not or could not turn them.

Tuscus knew that he was no different from them, in one sense. He, like they, was designed specifically for a job to be done. He and the few with the teachers were the only ones in his nursery who had been so designed, and they were better treated, but closer scrutinized. All that had meant to him thus far was that he had better food (which he had started sharing with Jen) and more of a chance of not waking up. It hadn't hit on him how different he really might be, at least not until he saw in the space of less than an hour four different humans bred for other tasks.

He wondered how come none of these creatures had been raised with him? He had been raised with the unaltered, but where were the nurseries that produced these tall three-eyes, these short five-eyes, the whistling fetus, the scoop-handed laborers? He had, in the past, seen the lumbering lifters from a distance, but they had seemed impossible to place on a human scale, as huge as they were. But these people, these were human like him in a way that Jen, though he looked similar, could not be. And he wondered, since he had been raised to believe the lifters were just insensate beasts, were the others here? He found that hard to believe, seeing them move in so human a manner, yet surely no one would let a sapient creature live in the middle of the boneyard. He was almost insane just from the smell and the flashes, in the short time he had been there. He could never last the rest of his life in it.

And then, what about the seven creatures that protected them, were they sapient? They acted as if they were, but they could just as easily be clever animals. If they weren't people, just human, could he be different? Was he an animal sent to live among people to mimic their ways sufficiently?

He already knew he was a mimic, after all, this is why he changed color to match his surroundings sometimes. Perhaps he changed personas to match the people around him. Perhaps he was not a person of his own, but a clever mimic. Perhaps he cared about Jen because he was unconsciously pretending to be him. And what of Jen? What was he bred for, why was he left apparently unaltered? Was Jen's heritage hidden, was Jen simply a more complex animal? Perhaps he was simply a tool, bred to socialize Tuscus and his ilk. Tuscus did not like thinking of these things. He wished he could stop.

They led him to a jumble of bones that forked the path. The pile only moderately stank. It was almost static, with a mild movement that could barely be seen. The three tall creatures, the three-eyes, moved some bones aside, revealing a passage, dark and edged by the bones, and Tuscus' teacher ushered him into the sharp dark, the sunlight from the now-risen Nod not being able to filter through the off-white sticks.

VII

Jen's Dream

He saw before him, in the night, a shifting figure, changing from old man, to young man, to old woman to young woman, changing features and stature. The figures shifted through everyone he had known, thought he had known, and could have conceived of knowing. He followed the figure, through a swamp, to a pressed dirt ramp that led up in the night.

The figure danced up the ramp, and he followed him. With one step, he crossed from night into day.

Before him, he saw a construction, a tower spiraling up into the sky. The air was suffused with light, with every atom shining from within. The brightest light came from the figure, which bounded up to the top of the tower, growing brighter and brighter the closer it approached to the tower's summit. When it rested there, the light pulsed to beyond the realm of his sight. He saw people around him, then, and he saw them all glowing from within, and they were living a life abliss. He felt joy wash over him, and he focused on the shifting figure on the tower, and he felt overwhelmed with love and peace.

VIII

A Boy with a New Family

Around dawn, maybe three hours later, Jen was woken up by noise as the teachers' door opened. Again, the young children gathered at the door, but only the light from the hall came through. Some remained in their bunks, Jen stayed where he was at the window, and he turned away from the door to look out again.

Boats sat half-sunk, or burnt, or empty, all motionless in the morning light. Buildings were listing in the water, some obviously sick or dead. A thick smoke rose from one or two, and flames sat just above the water in several places. The rope bridges connecting building to building, house to house, were cut and dangling down, floating on the water. People were climbing out of their windows, sitting on the rooftops and their pacing was the only movement. The boats sat as if still anchored, even the water rippled only where junk had fallen into it.

Through the door, men and women came through, young and old men and women, unfamiliar men and women, in what looked to be shells. The children who had gathered at the door pulled back from these kettle people, they weren't the teachers they had been expecting. They walked around, touching the children both carefully and roughly, testing them for bruises. They looked at the needle marks on the inside of their arms, and smiled at the children who were trying to squirm away from them.

They smiled uncomfortably, as if they had never seen children before, which they probably hadn't since their own days in the nursery. None of them were teachers, though they all had thought about it, otherwise they would not be sent to deal with the children. Their shells clicked as they walked, and when they had circumnavigated the room and looked over all the children, a few let their shells fall away to clatter on the floor. They hunched down, uncomfortably, as if they hadn't bent that way in days, to talked to the children in low soothing tones in a language the children couldn't understand.

One woman, the one who was standing at the door, watching the people who had dropped their shells, and who was still in her shell, noticed Jen as he sat at the window. She noticed that he did not try to move closer, that he seemed unwilling to join the groups clustering around the unshelled people. She moved to him and took his hand, and took him through the nursery's exit for the first time in his life.

IX

Over the Border and Safe for a While

On the day they stopped moving, when they crossed the new border between the Church and the Ducal Council, Tuscus saw his first Administrator. The fighting had stopped some days ago, and the teachers stopped in a field of corn near a small town, just on the other side of the newly revised border. They waited there, and two of the three-eyed beasts (he had learned that they were called myrmidons) had left them to run into the town, carrying a message from the eldest teacher. The farmers left them alone, for the most part, scooping the cornstalks into the lumbering thresher-cows that paced beside them.

A day and a night passed, and they fed on some of the older farmers that worked in the field, the constantly muttering creatures offering themselves up to the group. Tuscus was grateful for the meal – he hadn't had any meat in days. The children gathered some ears for themselves, and cooked the farmer's flesh with the corn. When the myrmidons returned, they carried a litter between them, bearing the Administrator.

Like most of the more specialized humans in Council territory, the Administrator was sexless and hairless. It wore warm robes, wrapped about it in layers, the folds holding its symbiotes. The head of the Administrator was the only part of its body visible, and the head held only a mouth, with two membranes where its ears would go and another membrane on its throat. The latter membrane let out a sharp hum, and the symbiotes, little sensor-rats, scrabbled out of the folds as quickly as they could, and crawled over the children. Tuscus did his best not to flinch as the dozens of eyes peered at him and the dozens of paws climbed through his clothes and against his skin. His teachers were speaking to the Administrator, but he did not hear what they were saying, though he tried. The sensor-rats kept distracting him, and letting out high-pitched whines from their torsos.

As quickly as they had come to the children, the sensor-rats left, and returned to the Administrators robes. Two myrmidons (Tuscus thought they were the same ones, but it was difficult to tell them apart) lifted the litter, and ran off toward the town.

The teachers came to Tuscus and the rest of the children and told them that they would be raised in this town, and that they would go no further. They said that the Administrator had deemed that they might be irreversibly contaminated by the templars, and, until they proved otherwise, they were to stay where they could do little harm. Tuscus knew better than to argue, for there was no appealing an Administrator's judgment. He saw the sense in it, and knew that he would do his best to prove his loyalty to the teachers that had saved him from the Sailor's Church.

As he was falling asleep that night, he found that he could not help wishing that they had been able to save Jen, too, but he knew that since the decision had been made, that was how it had to be. After all, the Administrator had no more freedom of thought than the farmers or the myrmidons. The Administrator could only make right decisions, all other options were closed to it. Tuscus was glad to know that such an animal was deciding his fate.

X

At the Seminary, Every Day Is Orientation Day

The gate to the basilica, the capital of the Sailor's Theocracy, was always open. There was a symbolic toll, the Church's first official moneymaker as a Church, and it had been used over the centuries to pay for additions to the original, already expansive building. The basilica soared and spread through the city that had grown around it, a city of churches, each one unique and beautiful, collectively the headquarters of all of the businesses of the nation.

At one end of the complex, east of the gate, there was the squat complex of the seminary. It was one of the oldest structures, originally built far away from the main buildings, in the slums that almost rested on land, but it had been slowly encroached upon by the ever-spreading basilica. Children from all the cities and towns in the Sailor's Church and the rest of the world came to the seminary. They came there to study, they came there to become the deacons, priests, and bishops who would run the businesses of the theocracy, and they came there because they didn't know where else to go.

An observer could always single out the ones from a newly conquered diocese, and there were a lot more of those these days. They always had a dazed look on their faces, or a determined set to their features obviously designed to put on a show of worldliness. Every child who had been raised in a Theocratic nursery would have no problem with gawking shamelessly as they entered the buildings which were famed the world over.

The central cathedral was always crowded. Every hour of the day, every day of the week, a long line wrapped around it. It was one of the few buildings in the city made completely of stone, and it was one of the largest buildings on the planet. Inside, it felt as if one was outdoors on a river on an overcast day. The walls had every inch covered with liturgical art: portraits of the Sailor's concubine; of the Patriarchs and Matriarchs; of bishops, priests, and deacons of note; of vast landscapes owned by the current Matriarch.

People said the cathedral had the entire history of the Sailor's Church in its art, but the one thing missing was an image of the Sailor. Instead, in the place of the altar, there was a pile of ceramic, brown and smooth, and from it emanated the voice of the Sailor. It never stopped speaking and it never repeated itself. One of the tasks of every student who attended the seminary was to spend a month transcribing their god's words, though it had been long since proven that they made sense only to one or two people in the audience at any given time. The words were always random prophecies for an individual's everyday life, and, more often than not, that person would be in the crowd to hear them.

Some said that the Sailor lived in the pile, but the bishops would take their prized students down, deep through the labyrinth under the cathedral, and, after two days of travel, the students would arrive at the Sailor's spartan crypt to spend a day with the god. Then they would return on a different two-day route, mute about what they had seen, even when they tried to describe it. The Sailor insisted on being surrounded by students and was never alone in the deep vault.

For Jen, this basilica was the greatest creation he could imagine, it was beyond possibility to him, and it overwhelmed him. He had seen pictures of it in the books that his liberators had brought, rough drawings that inspired him to study there, in such magnificence.

As far as he knew, his future in the Oligarchy had been undefined. He was one of the few who was theoretically a normal human, one of the few who had no real place in that society. He had always known that Tuscus had had a purpose, and he had felt lost next to his friend. He had felt that his sole purpose was to accompany Tuscus and provide him with companionship. The idea of his own purpose, separate from Tuscus, disturbed him. This basilica could have a place for him, this basilica could be where he could find his purpose. This huge monolith that was the basilica, it could be his place. This priesthood, it could be his new Tuscus.

The Rat in the Maze

Tuscus waited at the entrance to the blank, white hall. On the far side, he could see a bowl of steak and rice. In between, he knew something was waiting for him, but what, he didn't know.

Tuscus hadn't eaten in days. He was allowed water, although his teachers were threatening to cut that off as well. The problem was his coloring. He could not control it yet. He tended to change color with his emotions, something that the teachers did not approve of. They had tried every method they could think of, short of starvation, to train him to control his skin, but he still couldn't.

They had finally hit upon this method. He could eat the food, if he could get to it. To do so, he needed to cross this hall without being seen or heard. There were observers hiding in the seemingly empty hall, and they weren't too rough with him when they caught him. He had never made it past the second observer, his skin always flushed when he was excited or confident.

Tuscus swallowed and concentrated. His skin shifted from its normal reddish-brown (modeled on his memories of Jen's skin) to the stark white of the hallway. He sucked in a great breath and closed his nostrils. He stepped into the corridor. His irises changed to match his skin, leaving only his pupils hovering in mid-air.

He scrutinized the corridor, the currents of air. He took a step forward, then another, then another. He saw a distortion in the air, lying flat in the ground in front of him, and he carefully stepped over it. His lungs were getting tight.

The observer he had stepped over changed to a bright green, stood up, and smiled in his general direction before leaving down the corridor. Tuscus took advantage of this movement to cover is nose with his hand, open his nostrils and breathe. With his lungs full of fresh air again, he closed his nostrils and continued on.

The next observer was hanging from the ceiling, and he had no problem sneaking past her. She dropped down, turned green, and left, and again Tuscus breathed. He took a moment to stay still. He knew he was halfway through, and he knew that this was where he always screwed up. He did his best to settle his mind, and took his hands and pressed them against his stomach. The palms of his hands shifted through a rainbow of color as he bled off his excitement. With them still on his belly, he stepped forward.

The next observers he almost brushed into, as they were

leaning against the walls. He pulled his elbow back in time, and wavered as he went off balance. He caught himself, and stepped past him. They turned green and left and Tuscus breathed again.

Two more steps, three more, and he was at the food. He looked at it as best as he could from a step away. He couldn't sense anything. He put his hand over his nose and inhaled, but he only smelled steak and rice. He listened, but he only heard his own heartbeat. He reached forward, so hungry, and grasped the bowl, his hands coming into contact with the hands of the last observer, who turned blue, jerked the bowl away, and knocked Tuscus unconscious.

XII

Sometimes, You Just
Don't Notice the Years

The templar sat on the throne he had made, gazing at the cold light of the statue before him. He didn't argue with it anymore, not that he ever really had been able to. It spoke directly to him, and it was lonelier than he had ever been. It told him how it had lost all of its family so long ago that the stars had been different, and the Templar, who had never had a family, could say nothing to that. It told him again and again the story of the world as the statue saw it, from its isolated temple in an uninhabitable forest. The templar was enthralled and worshipped the ancient statue.

It claimed to have existed from when humans first set foot on Tubal-Cain, and it told many stories of humanity's fall from its grace into its current state. The statue promised to take care of the templar as long as the templar served it, and the templar had no ability to disagree. Every so often, the statue would direct a myrmidon to bring him food or take away his waste or change the throne's bedding. The beasts never walked between the statue and the templar, never interrupting the gaze.

When they ran low on supplies, the statue would send them out to raid a barge or two that drifted along the river located was an hour away. The area became known for piracy, though the myrmidons were always careful to kill everyone they waylaid. Eventually, the barge crews began to carry weapons, and the myrmidon's numbers began slipping. Still, they always managed to capture more than enough supplies to last them until the statue ordered the next raid.

Every week or so, the templar would get up and exercise, still looking at the blue-white light. The ice that had collected over his bare flesh would crackle and split, falling off as he exercised. After the ice had been completely shed, the templar would finally take his eyes off of the statue and go into a back room and sleep.

The myrmidons would clean up the ice, putting it into a bucket where it would melt. When the templar woke, he would take the bucket into the room where the helpless master of the myrmidons was held, and change the little kidnapped fetus-beast's slop bucket. Every time, the fetus-beast would try to control the templar, but he was too much in thrall to the statue, and the little creature's buzzing would merely annoy him. He would leave food and then return to his throne.

He would sit on the rough hewn wood, and it would stick into him in ways that he came to associate with contentment, staring deep at his god, the glowing statue, and the week would begin again.

XIII

Jen, a Bit Later

Brother Jenaro sat on the roof of the riverboat, sipping his water, fresh from the springs of Bensit on far Cigma, fortified with all the vitamins and minerals a human needs, no calories and no fat, only three denarii a serving (twelve on the riverboat), and watched the river Semt flow past him for the second time in his life. Even though he was headed upstream this time, the trip downstream had seemed much harder.

The bishopric of Nephi was paying for the trip, though not his food, and he had already spent half his remaining money on the salty water he drank. He was scared of the river water, even though he knew it was fine and the crew of the riverboat tended to drink it. Back at the seminary, the water around the school had always seemed foul, and, though he had acknowledged that it was potable, it just tasted the way Jen thought urine would taste like.

The riverboat was a luxury he wasn't used to, nor one he could afford. He couldn't even afford passage on one of the many barges they passed, towed up the river barely twice as fast as most people could walk. They had low, boxy shapes and were almost a boardwalk along the Semt, manned by couples with their apprentices camped on top, and their crews idly checking the ropes that pulled them upstream.

The riverboat sat alone in the middle of the river, four stories tall above the waterline, the river's edge far enough away that the barges drifting downstream could (and did) fit eight across passing on one side, sometimes coming a little too close for the barge-captains' taste, but not dangerously so. Music moved the floorboards under Jen's feet. Brother Tubret's band was putting on a show, and the drummers weren't yet out of sync. This was remarkable to Jen, who had lived next door to Tubret for the last three years, and had thought that arrhythmic white noise was the sound they had been going for. He supposed that hearing them through the deck of the riverboat had much to do with it. Most people on the boat were inexplicably watching them.

Tubret was going north from Nephi, along the Semt, and he claimed he was going to make his fortune performing and proselytizing at the mining camp at the head of the Nephi, where meteoric iron had been found at the bottom of the crater lake Sali. The miners were starved for entertainment and glutted of money, and hopefully amiable to his music. Tubret had hoped that he could afford the trip by playing on the boats he booked passage on, though he was still in debt for the riverboat's ticket. Jen, as far as he knew, was only going as far as Nephi, though the bishopric there had said they had special instructions for him.

Jenaro had been out of seminary for half a year. He had been brought there when he had been rescued from that horrible nursery, or so he was always told. His memories of the nursery were quite fond, and he would sometimes dream, late at night, of sitting next to Tuscus, playing games and talking. Even so, he was thankful, and he did love his job, he felt it was his true calling, even if he hated making money, the true and objective measure of holiness.

Unlike his fellow graduates, he had not been apprenticed yet and he did not really desire to be. He wanted to stay around the school. He was a constant bother to his former instructors, though they were nice enough not to admit it to his face. He lived on what he could and money wasn't as much a problem for him as he wished it would be, an attitude he kept from himself and others. He had great facility for turning anything he was doing into profit. He wished it were more difficult, he told himself, so he could feel that he had earned it.

As things stood, he constantly felt guilty about his ability, and he had great difficulty disposing of the money he so rapidly accumulated. He couldn't give it away, it would insult the recipient. He wouldn't buy luxury goods, he didn't want them, he didn't know what to do with them, and he found them to be ostentatious. He knew it was his duty to make money, and that his ability to do so so readily was a sure sign of the Sailor's favor, but still, it bothered him.

He had been thankful when the bishopric of Nephi had called him up. There was no way that he could prosper there.

After all, it was his hometown, and hometowns are remarkably tough to get a good start in, especially after you forsake it for the big city. People who had remained back home tended not to like that. And the opportunities couldn't be that good. The current bishop had been there since it had been taken from the Ducal Council, a full fifteen years, and she had not been able to expand it into an archdiocese. If a bishop couldn't make money, then obviously inexperienced Jen couldn't, or so he hoped as he watched the barges slip past him. He idly wondered, with the eye of a future priest, how much profit they were pulling in, how much overhead went into bedding and boarding the deck hands, keeping the boat repaired and paying docking fees.

Tubret finished had finished his set, and he came up to sit next to Jenaro. Jen's eyes were closed a bit against the sun.

"Good show," Jen lied, "Here." He tossed Tubret almost all of the rest of his money.

"What's this for?" Tubret asked.

"You did a good job. I think I should pay you for it."

"I don't need your money. I got plenty from just now." Tubret shoved the money back into Jen's hand.

"Take it. You earned it. I don't need it."

"I get your cast offs now? I didn't take them when we were neighbors, I don't take them now. You take your money and throw it overboard." Tubret stalked off the deck, thumping his feet hard, just to make sure Jen heard him.

Jen watched him go, then he rose up and went down to the commissary, where he bought more mineral water and was left with nothing but his clothes on his back.

XIV

Jen, Back in His Hometown

Nephi might have been his hometown, but he had never left the nursery in all his years growing up there. He knew better than to gawk as the riverboat pulled into its dock, but he was filled with a feeling of awe and homecoming. The town didn't impress him so much as seem quaint. At the seminary, he had been in the middle of a city of five million, here, in Nephi, the population peaked at a hundred thousand, and only twenty thousand were permanent residents. The rest were miners on leave, merchants stopping over for the night, and tourists hoping for a bit of the unspoiled. They were disappointed. When the Pondscum Guide to Nod had been published, five years back, it had listed Nephi as the haven for those seeking a quiet little backwater. Naturally, by the next year, three casinos, twelve commercial museums, a zoo, and Sailor-knew-how-many souvenir shops had opened.

Even so, the transient population tended to be barge crews, running food, mail, and miscellany up to the miners and steel back down.

The old town hall had been converted into the cathedral. A museum to the evils of the Oligarchs in its basement was a popular attraction. It was the best place for it, even if the windows into the water had been boarded up at the request of the bishop, ever since they started to leak. The cathedral's vaults were said to be amongst the strongest in the region, converted from the treasury of the old government.

The bishop's office, on the sixth story, covered a third of the floor. Jenaro was asked to sit outside in the waiting room, though his appointment came and passed. The secretary, a priest who had lived in Nephi from the beginning of the occupation and come there with the bishop, did not seem to hold any regard for Jen. He came up to the desk to speak to the secretary, but every time, he was ignored. He spent his time reading the commentaries placed on every flat surface possible, texts the bishop had written, apparently at the expense of her advancement in the church.

Jen had tried to read a few of these texts on the riverboat. They had only cost him twenty denarii for the complete set, and he had found no shortage of people willing to sell theirs when he had asked, but he had thrown them overboard by the end of the first day. They were uniformly dull and pedantic, the only interesting parts the too-few anecdotes of the early conversion of Nephi, which Jen liked primarily for their background into his hometown.

Few people knew that she had tried to fill the entire text

with those anecdotes. That is what she had sent in to her editors. Instead, they had replaced the more sensitive bits, which seemed in many cases to be most of the books, with thousand year-old commentaries from Luidprand, a minor Patriarch who had fallen out of favor upon his death at the hands of his mistress. The bishop had given up trying to write anything original and was now just happy to be allowed to keep her job. If Jenaro had been paying more attention to the books he was browsing in her waiting room, he would have noticed that these, the original manuscripts, held a much more interesting account of the night Tuscus was stolen from him.

Before he could really get into the books, the secretary summoned Jen, and he entered into the bishop's office. She sat behind a broad wood desk, made of houseplant, clean save for a single sheet of paper. There was only one chair in the room, and she was sitting in it. He wondered if she made other merchants and priests stand, if that helped her intimidate them. He insisted to himself that he wasn't going to be cowed, that he would be sure of himself as he stood rocking back and forth, slowly, on his heels. She was looking at him, and she did not blink.

"Sit," she said, and he sat down, cross-legged, on the carpet, which moved slowly under his legs, a sign that it hadn't been groomed in a while. "You know of a man named Tuscus? He came from the nursery here. He came from the one that you were rescued from. He disappeared the night we liberated Nephi." She knew Jen knew Tuscus, but she wanted to see if he admitted it.

"I did, but it was fifteen years ago. I have not heard from him since then."

"You remember him? You know him well?"

"Yes. Yes, I did. Fifteen years ago."

She spoke flatly. "You have enough of a connection. Tuscus is back in town now. He is working for a firm that runs supplies up to the miners. He is an Council citizen. He will need a priestly escort."

"You want me to be it? I haven't done anything like that before."

"So? You are now in my diocese. You are under my wing. I want you to watch him for anything you think is odd. This time is the first time he's been back to Nephi since he was stolen from us. This time is the first time he's been in the Sailor's territory, actually. You leave on his barge tomorrow. You are staying where, meantime?"

"I was hoping I could stay here."

"You don't have any money?" she asked.

Jen shook his head.

She looked at him with disgust.

Jenaro went off to his cell, a small closet in the northwest corner on the first floor, where he curled up into a naked ball and fell asleep, his shirt and pants his pillow.

XV

Tuscus Comes Home

Tuscus looked over the papers for the nth time. His instructions were very simple. He had received them in a note written in block letters and small words. He was to be a courier. He was to deliver an envelope and then return home, no more, no less. The message had come with a pile of money, which scared Tuscus every time he looked at it. Because of that pile, he knew that he was going to be audited when he was done. He had heard what happened to people who failed their audits. Some say that the administrators in the Oligarchy were the ones to be feared, but he knew that the accountants were really the ones he needed to be worried about. He had seen people who weren't deemed to be cost effective, and he had seen how they had died. It was painless, but they were still dead.

He knew, on the surface, that he should be grateful for

such efficiency, that it kept the Oligarchy strong, but he was scared of death. He knew that if he failed once too often, or once too drastically, that they would weigh his training, his food, his lodging, his inoculations, everything, and he would be found wanting. He knew that this was how most people in his profession died. Not by assassination, or caught and killed in the Theocracy's prisons. This was the common belief, but he knew enough about the Sailor's Church to know it didn't do that. It was also concerned about cost-effectiveness. Instead of killing them, it used old Council agents as tools, either brainwashing them and sending them back to the Oligarchy or enslaving them in the underground farms that kept their nurseries fed.

It was more common to die because of an internal audit, the one that everyone with an ounce of sense feared. He had sat in on two in his life, and those two had been the most rational experiences he could remember. Both times he could follow the math, which he usually wasn't good at, but they made it so clear, going nice and slow over the equations, over the records, line by line processing of the numbers. He had almost wanted to become an accountant by the end of both audits, and both times he had ended up agreeing, as did the subjects, that they simply were pulling in more resources than they contributed, and it wasn't fair to the rest of the people of the Ducal Council that their resources, their hard labor, be allocated to support this drain upon the society.

This was Tuscus' first mission, and it was his first real attempt to prove his worth. He knew that they had invested a lot in him. They reminded him constantly of how he had been rescued from the Church when they had come to steal Nephi, how very good teachers had died for him. They reminded him of how they had spent twenty-six years educating him, making him the best they could, given the flawed material they had to work with, how even his geneset was special, and how they spent so many hours trying to get him viable, how he was the only one of his geneset to be born and how there would be no more of his type if he failed.

Of course, they did this to everyone, with different stories in case they ever talked to each other, but always consistent with the subject's private fears. Where those thoughts weren't exploitable, they made them so. This had been successfully done to Tuscus, even though only one of his teachers had died, and that had been caused by food poisoning from eating raw fish five years after Tuscus had been rescued.

It was common practice on the first mission, or so the rumors said, and Tuscus believed them, that a senior agent would be watching him, and that this agent was to kill him if he did anything that agent deemed inappropriate to the mission. Tuscus would never know who this agent was, but that the agent would testify at the inevitable audit that follows a first mission, in the rare event that Tuscus survived.

If he survived the mission, and the senior agent didn't kill him, he would pass the audit. Tuscus was never told this, he suspected it and tried to start it as a rumor several times, just to hear some reassurance out of the grapevine. It always came back to him that even if he survived the mission, and the agent, odds are he wouldn't last out the audit. He didn't realize it, but the rumors were planted and monitored just as readily as his memories. The reality was far different - the audit was everything, and, though there was a supervising agent, they could only report, not act.

He had arrived in Nephi just that morning and had found his crew without any trouble. The paperwork to get into the city had taken several months, but he supposed his cover was good enough, because they finally let him in. It wasn't, but then, he was spending a lot of Council money, more than he realized, and he wasn't going to be taking of it back, the Bishop's tariffs levied against him would make certain of that. Since coming into the city had been such a hassle, he was not ready for the ease he had moving around his hometown.

Part of the problem was that Oligarchy's citizens had no economic training. They did not need it in a command economy such as theirs. With a structure as complex and tightly planned as it was, only those specially designed for the job could handle the numbers, anyone else (including the Sailor's spies, until they just gave up and fed the data to the Sailor, as it needed a god's analysis) just grew more and more frustrated trying to understand how such a precariously balanced system could work for a week, much less the millennia it had.

His captain, Jak, took him to lunch, and told him of her past. He already knew that she was forty-two and her husband (and former apprentice) was her first mate. She had unknowingly worked for the Ducal Council four times in her career, eight, just as unknowingly, for the Church, as far as Tuscus had been made aware of. He did not know that her first job for the Sailor, the one and only one she was aware that she did, was smuggling the armor to the Theocracy templars as they waited around Nephi on the night of the invasion. He knew that she was content to own her own boat, and not go farther than that. He had also been told that she would not be the senior agent, absolutely not. Maybe.

She told him how that her employers, his corporation, had hired two extra hands for her barge, she said that they had done so to make certain they got to Lake Sali in time, which struck Tuscus as odd, primarily because of the time it took to get him into the country. He failed to realize then, though he eventually did later, that if he hadn't been available, someone else would have been, and the delivery would be done just as efficiently, if not more so, by someone else.

He gave her money for supplies out of his corporate expense account, or so he told her, and he admonished her that he must have receipts. After she left, he spent the day alone in his old hometown. Like Jenaro, he had not ever been back to Nephi, but, unlike Jen, he had never been to any city before. He had spent his entire life in one training camp after another, and his experience with anything outside of those little hamlets was nonexistent. He wandered from rooftop to rooftop, stopping and staring every time he crossed one of the rope bridges connecting the buildings to each other. The last time he had seen anything so populous and so busy had been during those forbidden peeks through the window of the nursery, which he deliberately avoided thinking of, scared of what he might find and what he might remember. So many different sorts of people, to him, and they were all of the same caste, something he had had a hard time grasping when he was studying the Sailor's Church.

Tuscus was of the middle caste in the Oligarchy, and he thought of himself as such. It held more power than any of the other, non-administrative castes, and he was proud to be in it. There was not too much responsibility, but enough, and his thoughts weren't too impaired. He could pass for a normal human, primarily because he had finally learned to control the way the colors flowed in his skin.

In the past two years, as his graduation grew closer and closer, he tended to turn from a carefully cultivated deep brown, a color he had picked because it reminded him of Jenaro, (he told no one this, and Jen was actually a bit redder), to a bright green, though only on his chest and back, so most people never saw it. He always wore shirts so it wouldn't give him away, even when he was horribly hot or etiquette called for him to be bare-chested. He explained that his birthing had gone wrong and he was horribly embarrassed by it, and to please not call attention to the fact.

In his studies of the Church, he had always wondered how anyone could get any work done, especially hard, essential work like farming and manufacturing, without any caste structure to mandate who did what. He would never do any farming, and he couldn't believe that the men he was shipping food to were mining out of their own free will.

He refused to believe that, given the choice to do anything, they would sink themselves deep underground, tunnel under a lake, and extract the iron from beneath it in those dripping tunnels where the lake could crash down and kill them all instantly. It was beyond his understanding, no matter how much money they were paid. Of course, these same men would look at Tuscus' job of being a spy and assassin, (though he had not really killed anybody yet, except in practice, and that didn't count, since his victims had been literally born and bred for it), and think him crazy. He would contend that they were right to think so, since he had been made so he had to be a spy, and he couldn't be anything else, and he had been made special because no one in their right mind would chose his line of work.

He ate dinner alone in the same market he had gone to to buy his clothes and books. He realized that if he was going to play the merchant, he had better look the part, especially after the odd looks that Jak had given him when he introduced himself. He charged it all to his expense account. He was starting to get used to the idea, and besides, he could justify it as part of his cover, and they wanted him to go undetected, didn't they? The plain gray pants and shirt that he had come with, that they had given him and had been his uniform all his life simply wouldn't cut it any more. He bought clothes that he thought a merchant would wear, a bright red shirt with blue stars under the armpits, and a pair of white shorts, horizontally striped in the same blue as the stars, both covered in bright patches at jaunty angles, a matching he thought to be rather clever.

He ate dinner and returned to the boat. It was a medium sized barge, basically a box on top of a hull. The cargo, his cover, really, was on the dock, three crates of refrigerated food, a crate of mail, and a crate of inoculations.

Due to the rampant biological warfare between the Ducal Council and the Sailor's Church, people living near either country had to go in for their inoculations at least once a month, preferably once a week. Most people died, not of old age directly, but when their bodies could no longer handle the drugs and counterphages that flooded their systems.

Usually one died from one of the plagues the other side was constantly releasing or an allergic reaction to the antipathogens that the side you were on was responding with, and usually when you were in your early hundreds. It took an incredible constitution to survive much longer, though it was rumored that one or two of the autarks was over two hundred. No one knew how old the Matriarch was, although everyone correctly assumed that she was fairly middle-aged.

All of the cargo had been bought for him by the Council at no cost to him, purchased through his expense account, and provided with the boat. He sat in the hull, and his quarters, with everyone else's, were in the communal room above it, his partition was separated by curtain from the rest of the crew. He crawled in, bundled up his old clothing, and checked the envelope carrying the message. He had taped it to his stomach. It was rather thick and poked him when he bent at the waist, but he thought it was the safest place for it.

And so he went to sleep, and he did not see the small, bald man. The back of the man's skull was new flesh where a tattoo had been removed, though the grafting was good enough that it simply caused his skin not to pucker as much when he looked up. The bald man's skin became black-speckled gray to match the shadows. He looked over Tuscus, running his hands under his shirt and smoothly, painlessly, peeling back the tape holding the envelope in place.

XVI

A Sourpuss on the Boat

Fennish turned the envelope over and over in his hands as he sat in his bunk. Unconsciously, his skin had slipped back into its normal color, a pale gray-brown, though his scar tissue on the back of his head was a more rich brown. He had quite a bit of trouble with getting it the right color, in part because the skin was newer, but mostly because he couldn't see it and he never knew if it was behaving. He spent hours with pairs of mirrors trying his best, but it always reverted when he wasn't looking.

The envelope was rather plain and sealed in an inconspicuous manner. It looked like it was simply taped shut, but Fennish knew from opening many like it that no matter how he opened it, the envelope would dissolve when its contents were taken out. The address, naturally enough, was missing. There was nothing about it, no markings of any kind, that could serve to distinguish it from any other envelope he had come across, except by its sheer lack of distinction.

He had been toying with the idea of replacing it with a substitute, but no, that could cause more trouble than he already had to deal with. The boy was completely incompetent, he thought. He could simply throw the envelope over board, but he didn't think too seriously of that, as he knew that it had to be delivered, he just did not want to trust such a witless infant with it.

Never, in all his days, had the charge lost the package so early. Usually, the kid lost it on the third day, around lunchtime, but this one, this one was a complete waste. No one could be that lax or that stupid. Of course, Fennish had gotten more impatient and more intolerant as the years went by, as well as better at what he did. Only twice before had he bothered the children by going through his charge on the first day after he had met them, and never before had he done so in their sleep. Fennish was going to make sure that the child could never endanger anyone through his gross stupidity.

XVII

Being Woken by Someone
Banging on Your Home

Jenaro arrived at the barge early in the day, before anyone on it was up. Jen had eaten at the cathedral, the grub put out for the poor, and the bishop had stared at him until he put it down and left. He knocked on the hatch, but lightly, not wanting to start off on a bad foot by waking anyone up. He waited, but there was no answer. He climbed up on the roof of the crew's cabin and sat on its edge, his feet swinging a little, occasionally accidentally kicking the side of the cabin. He didn't wake anyone up, but the dreams inside the boat became uniformly strange, giants striding over the forests, peglegged beasts chasing the dreamer, and one half-memory, the dreamer locked in a padded basket with quiet voices and loud footsteps the only things he could perceive.

The sun was still low in the sky, not yet above the buildings in the lake that surrounded them, and Jen was in shadow, a feeling he didn't mind at all. It was nicely cool, and he watched the lifters haul their cargo to the marketplace on their table-like backs, their long arms pushing against the ground every third step or so, men guiding them along the rope bridges. The handlers would reach up with a long hook and poke a thigh or pull the long hair that so often got caught in the lifter's eyes if its owner didn't shave their heads. He heard the low singing of the merchants warming up their voices for out-calling each other in the open market, and the background noise became a thrum of voices, occasionally pierced by a louder call when one got the advantage of his neighbors and dominated the octave.

The traffic grew heavier, than quickly lighter, and then the sun was over the buildings, right into Jen's eyes, and he blinked at it, but it felt good on his skin, even so. The air was a bit cooler than he was used to, but this was to be expected, considering how far north he was from where he had spent his seminary years. It wasn't too bad, he must have still been a bit acclimatized for the years he spent here at as a child, and so he enjoyed it, with the occasional shiver.

XVIII

Yawn

Jak opened the hatch to her quarters to see the priest sitting on the roof. To her, he looked like every other priest she had ever had on these trips, all young, all completely inexperienced, fresh out of seminary, all too stupid still to refuse obviously pointless, profitless assignments. Even so, she had encountered two who had surprised her and raised graft to brilliant heights, and she was quite impressed with the way they had turned such a crap job into their stake for bigger and better assignments. She doubted that this one, who looked so young, even though he was older than the others had been, would be doing anywhere near the same.

She did not really resent the law that required the priests to oversee any transaction. It kept everyone honest enough, though she trusted her apprentices as much as she trusted herself to do what was best for the boat. She needed someone to oversee the numbers aspect, which she wasn't at all good at, not anymore, though she had been in her youth, but she hated doing it so much she forced herself to forget. Normally, her husband would handle the books (that was about all he was good for, she would tell him in those more tense moments, and he wasn't even that good at that) but it was always nice to have a priest check things over. If they skimmed off the top, well, that was the fee she paid and it was well worth it. She would have had to pay more to have a professional accountant do it, and she would lose more if she had to rely on her husband.

Sailor forbid she was going to trust the company which had hired her, or that incompetent little punk they had sent along to watch her. She introduced herself to the priest, who had yet to see her, though he must have heard her, because he did not look at all startled to hear her greeting. He was not terribly talkative, and absolutely awful at small talk, but he smiled a lot, and he seemed sincere when he did it. He spoke with a Council accent, just like the merchant did. She had always found it to be too verbose, like they couldn't focus a thought, but she didn't say anything, and she could almost understand everything he was saying. When she asked him about his bookcooking skills, he just waved his hands about and tried not to talk and he looked embarrassed.

XIX

An Educational Interlude

It struck the early biologists as odd that there was a class of creatures on Nod that was unrelated to any of the others. It was very clear that humans were closely related to the rats and dogs and cows, and even the chickens and the corn and the potatoes. But the gene structure of everything else was so different as to be unrecognizable. For a centuries after the structure of genes in humans and like beings, classed as helical, after their DNA's shape, was understood, a similar attempt had been fruitless to find it in the other flora and fauna.

But then, after a time, the three rings that were duplicates of each other and had been thought to be an oddly complex plasmid, was recognized as the genetic code of most of the life on the planet. Those creatures were called ringed for the shape of the encodings. And with that, the biologists realized just how rare and unique the helical beings were.

This did not come as a surprise to the Theocracy or worshipers of the Ship, who had always contended that helicals had been brought to Tubal-Cain on the Ship. The Ducal Council was only a confederation that opposed to the Sailor's Church at that time, the autarks still being unmodified humans and not the divine Administrators that they would later become. Their power was still based in their duchies and nurseries, not in their sheer will over their people as it would be later.

The Council researchers were ordered to keep the discovery from the public, but telling a scientist to be quiet about a discovery is as effective as telling a fish to breathe air. It's a trait which has stayed the same across all human cultures and all of history - no secret remain a secret once it is known by an academic. Some would consider this one of the greatest survival traits that humanity has. The news was out across the world within a week of the peer reviews. There was much rejoicing, and then much research into the effects.

After all, all the land animals were helical, and the only terrestrial ringed life were the plants that composed the vast forests. The only mobile ringed life were the fish that inhabited the waters, and those only at great depths. There were no great fossils of any surface animal, only layers of ash and fossilized seeds. These layers of ash, as well as the exceedingly protected seeds of the land plants and the poorly protected ones of the submerged plants and the new (for them) discipline of astronomy provided a clue. It seemed that Nod was variable star, and there was a burst of activity every fifty thousand years. It also seemed that Cain's orbit was a bit eccentric, a fact already known, as the rainy season's cloud cover kept the moon warm as it swung away from the star. The combination of Nod's aggravation and Tubal-Cain being on the wrong side of its primary at the wrong time served to regularly scour the planet of any life on the surface.

A panic ensued, as traditionally happens at such times, until it was finally expressed that the next event would happen in forty thousand years, which was long enough for anyone's comfort. And so, it was forgotten about by the general populace, but the research that the panic started continued, as it had proven profitable. For example, it was revealed that the helical creatures, the ones easily digestible, were all directly related to each other. The differences between a human and a cow, or rat, or chicken, were negligible. To a great extent, they might as well have been the same species, diverging at a common ancestor, its remains buried beneath the ash. Those worshipers of the Ship or the Sailor again pointed to their faith as the answer, others, not willing to give scientific backing to a religion, especially one so obnoxiously expansive, wrote off the ancestor to the burn-offs.

But there was a lot of debate as to why the differences existed at all. And, more to the point, why the helical species couldn't reproduce naturally, at least not the way the other species did. The plants tended to be fine, it was true, but it was risky not to closely supervise them, and wise to prevent them from spawning, as mutations became rampant very shortly. The great corn forest on Lido Island was proof of that - no one had entered it and lived in over one and a half thousand years. Recent aerial surveys still showed no break in the giant green and yellow stalks that moved too much like the other, nonhelical, plant life.

The best bet was to incubate the embryos, fetuses, and young children underground or underwater. There, at least, the nurseries could operate effectively. Attempts to bring them closer to the surface resulted in miscarriage and deformity. The nurseries required constant supervision, as did the in vitro and decanted children, and the whole process was by no means cheap. Some attempts were made to breed in vivo, but the animals were sterile not long after walking on the surface for the first time. A subterranean life was not tolerable to the livestock either, and so the nurseries were the only solution.

XX

Tuscus Wakes

Tuscus rose, woken up by the thrum of the cable, a long chord strung to the hull, singing under the mass of the boat as the motors dragged the barge upstream on it. He lay there in the cabin, his eyes still grainy from the sleep, and listened to the noise, trying to figure out what it was, trying to place it in his mind, but not really succeeding until he crawled out and into the sun where he saw the river pass by slowly under him. Trees, thick and clustered, composed the shore, fighting each other for the water and the debris that floated down it, only for it to get caught in their roots and decompose. Stumps rose in the shallower parts of the river, dead trees that had grown out too far and had drowned, decomposing to feed their less adventuresome counterparts. Just as Tuscus knew not to eat anything from or near the native plants (some oozed sap which would kill a man), these trees somehow knew not to attack humans, though how they had learned the lesson, no one had ever known.

The river was deserted, the only activity the perpetual writhing of the poison jungle. There were no other barges ahead. He couldn't see behind, but there wasn't anyone to see there either. On the deck, the priest, who looked a bit familiar, was playing cards with Jak and her husband.

The priest had the majority of the money in front of him. He had started with nothing, but they had insisted on paying him for looking over their books. He had done that earlier, and he didn't really do anything but check the math, which had been okay for the most part, as far as he could tell. He had always loved going over the numbers, and if he could take being inside an office all his life, he would have become an accountant. The money was easier to deal with if he thought of it simply as numbers on paper, the abstraction made him far less queasy than the real thing.

He had tried to prevent them from paying him, but he didn't want to insult them, so he had proposed the card game they were playing in an effort to have them win it back from him, but that simply wasn't working. Their cards were always worse than his, no matter how hard he tried to lose. He had started folding, but they had caught on, or so he feared, and he didn't want them hating him from the first moments of the trip, so he he was looking quite embarrassed about it.

Jak's eldest apprentice was checking the rope the barge ran along, keeping the pulley clear and making sure the incoming rope was free of knots. The younger apprentice was below rearranging the cargo. He heard her grunt and swear as she heaved the crates about, ostensibly to balance the load. Jak had given her the job as make-work, and there was nothing she could do but get stronger shoving the crates about. The crates weren't heavy enough to throw the barge off by much, though the occasional radical shift caused great problems for the other apprentice as the boat would lurch to one side quickly.

The priest stared at Tuscus, not making the effort to look away, he stared at him as if he was seeing him, not for the first time, but as if his face was familiar. The priest realized that he was staring, blushed, and turned quickly away. Tuscus then recognized him and looked away also, pressing his hands to his belly.

Something felt wrong. Tuscus felt under his shirt, scratching under his arms, his chest, and then his belly, when he noticed that there was no envelope. He crawled back into the cabin as quickly as he could, almost kneeing the gray-brown man curled up against the wall. He searched his bunk, where he found nothing, just what he had brought on board. He tore through the bunk, he stripped naked, he ripped everything from the wall, he rummaged through the rooms beside his, separated by the curtains, and he found nothing, though he knew he wouldn't, and then he did it again and again and again, until his luggage and his neighbors' luggage was thrown everywhere.

One set must have belonged to the priest, for all there was in it was a change of clothes and a book, rather thick, filled with writing which he couldn't read, or he didn't try. If he had given it more time, he would have found it wasn't in a different language, though it was to most people who looked at it, since it was the one that Jen had been brought up in, and learning Oligarch if you were in the Theocracy had only recently come back into fashion.

Jen had started the journal when it could it be dangerous to write in Oligarch, hoping in part that he would be caught and fined. No matter how he left it open in his supervisor's office, that never happened, in no small part because the handwriting was horrible, all vertical with no real space between characters and blurred together.

Fennish didn't wake during this, he knew the search would happen (it always did) and he knew how to sleep through such things. He knew the envelope was safely hid where Tuscus would never find it, floating on a plate in an upside down, airtight basket tied under the hull, and he could get to it quick enough if necessary. The entire cabin was torn through with nothing left alone, and then Tuscus began to sob, quietly, seeing his own death so early into the trip. Not that his death wasn't the right decision, he knew, on the intellectual level, because he had wasted their training and if he couldn't do this one simple task, how was he to help his country that had paid so much for him? As he sobbed, he tried to put back what he had destroyed, but he wasn't really concerned with what the others would say, since he was dead regardless.

As he cried, quietly, but it was so loud to him, he didn't hear the thrumming of the rope stop, he didn't hear the cries as it went slack and slithered through the water, through the gears of the pulley and cranks. The end, cut smoothly but fraying more, caught on the motor as it turned, pulling the rope only part of the way through before the ends stuck in the box and the motor froze up.

He did feel the lurch as the barge stopped as its motor did, and the statues he had been replacing to their original position in an apprentice's bunk, one of each of the woman's household gods, fell off. Though he was to pretend to be a member of the faithful during this trip, and he had read up on it, he never had, nor ever would, understand it. The idols flew into him, and scratched him hard with their pointed heads and feet, bruising him where they fell sideways into him. Fennish saw this, and left the cabin quietly, his skin graft on the back of his head a bright red flush, glowing as he climbed through the deck door onto the surface of the boat.

XXI

The Boat Stopped

Jenaro grabbed for his money as the boat lurched and tumbled into Jak's husband. Later he would regret this, and thought that he should have put it into Jak's pile while they all were tumbling, but then he felt even guiltier for thinking this, giving up his winnings so easily, so he just stopped dwelling on it altogether, which turned out to be healthier in the long run. He saw the elder apprentice pull his hand out of the motor, holding it tight and wrinkled in his other hand, and he saw the boat start to swing towards the shore, the river growing shallower and shallower. More and more roots stuck up and scraped into the hull, and the barge bounced up through the water, turned sideways to the current, and drifted, more slowly now, towards the shore and downstream, to get fouled on a tighter collection of the roots and come to a halt.

He saw Fennish climb out of the cabin, though he did not

know Fennish yet, had not even met him, had ignored him when he went into the cabin to put his stuff away, and though the captain had made a point of introducing his sleeping body, he had not learned the man's name. He saw Fennish clamber onto the roof, a handbow in his grasp. Where he had gotten it, no one ever found out, because afterward, when all the handbows were accounted for, they supposed he took it on board with him, though no one knew where he could have kept it. The small man stood up as tall as he could, his eyes looking calmly along both shores, through the trees that lined them, in the roots that touched the water, curled up, and he stood there while the Jen collected himself.

To calm himself, Jen put away the cards so slowly, so carefully, concentrating on them. The apprentice had taken off the motor housing, with Jak standing next to him, watching quietly, and her husband gone into the hold to check on the other, younger apprentice, who had been quiet for the first time since she went down into the hold. Fennish lowered himself from the cabin's roof, walked to the edge of the hull, stood on it, his toes curled on the corner, gripping it tight, his heels hanging in the air. Jen watched Fennish stand there, watched him watching with his handbow raised, and saw the arrow sprout from his back, and another and another and another, at least six in a perfect hexagon, tight in his back, and his toes slipped, and his feet slid down the inside of the hull, and Fennish tilted forward, his knees seeming to bend the wrong way, and fell off the boat.

Jenaro stared where Fennish had been. He never knew his name, never would, never spoke to him, never would, the man was there and then gone, probably hadn't even been paid yet, these were the thoughts that he had. He couldn't move, didn't think to move. Jak yelled at him, and he heard her, but he couldn't listen to her, she wasn't anything he could think about. She grabbed his arm and pulled him, behind the apprentice, into the hold.

XXII

Burrow Into the Boat

Tuscus saw them all climb in, and he saw the man, the priest, in Jak's grip, and he recognized the expression on the man, the fear he had seen, the fear that had hidden behind the reassuring whispers so long ago, the fear of a man who couldn't understand violence caught in the middle of it. Sure, Jenaro had seen, time and again, his friends in the nursery die, but they died quietly, in their sleep, for a greater cause, so he was told and so he believed at the time. When he joined the seminary, and found that the Church didn't do the same, he learned to count it amongst the other barbarities of the Ducal Council. But that greater cause served everyone in the Oligarchy, so he was taught then, and it was true that the denizens of the Council led healthier, more robust lives than their counterparts. It was the only one he remembered that was true, but this was never something he questioned - any nation that killed its children for design flaws, he was told, was capable of any evil, even if the people in the Oligarchy had no real concept of the individual, all of which of course made him more happy to be in seminary. This was a perpetual argument between the two nations as to which were happier - a group living a life that they chose or a group living a life they were designed for.

This fear made Tuscus finally forget his lost message, and he realized that here, in front of him, crawling awkwardly behind Jak through the hatch was the man he had dreamed of quietly, for he knew better than to tell anybody, the man who had held his hand so many nights as a child as they both fell asleep, faces close together, whispering, and this man, this one he had thrown so much on, had modeled his skin on. He saw now he would have to add a bit more red, but he didn't know just how much he would have to add to the mix, mainly because it was so dark in the cabin, and Jen was climbing through the light. This man was a priest, a priest of the Sailor, his opposite in the Church. He was one who kept that evil going, one who dedicated his life to using everyone and everything for his own advancement, with no consideration of the effects on anyone else, the rest of society or the nation, anything but the self. Jak closed and locked the hatch to the outside as best as she could, but the latch didn't look too sturdy.

"Shit, shit, shit" Jak was chanting, under her breath, her hand pulling out a steel dagger from under her bunk. She had hid it there, long ago, in the years right after she had bought the boat. She had saved a full year to buy that dagger, and when she had almost lost the boat, four years before, in that year when the river nearly dried up, she used it as collateral in the loan that kept her alive and allowed her to use the boat when the waters returned. The Matriarch, at great personal cost (not really, because she took a cut out of every thing that went up or down the river for the next year and came out far ahead, one more reason she was the Matriarch), had had clouds seeded every day for three months and water poured from Lake Sali, until the river had reached its proper level. Her husband knew about the dagger, but had never seen it, but they had planned on giving it to her eldest apprentice when Jak died. The priest, Jen, was praying under his breath, but not really, though he should have been, instead, he was repeating over and over again, "I don't want to die, I can't die, I will die." Perhaps it was a prayer after all.

A thump-thump-thump hit the wall of the barge, a thump-thump-thump on the left side and right side of the barge, simultaneous thump, close together, directly across from each other, six sharp, quick knocks.

Tuscus took his hands out, covered them by wringing them, trying to redirect the drugs coursing into his veins from the glands implanted in his body. The drugs had been blamed for a few deaths, some Tuscus had seen, once simply because a lifter had been given an overdose as a demonstration, and then told to erect a foundation from cement slabs. It did so, but it was dead before it was able to sink the last pylon into the water, when the chemicals had flooded the system, causing it to overload at the most inconvenient times. The body was consumed in a great burst of energy, leaving only an emaciated bag of skin and bones ripped into shreds. But then, people without such self-control deserved such fates, so he had been taught. He was glad that the darkness obscured the way his skin was shifting color. Everyone else noticed, but thought they were hallucinating under the stress, they couldn't miss a shift from a light gray to near black and back again in splotches, even in the cabin's low light.

Another thump-thump-thump, thump-thump-thump, and then a new sound, feet landing hard above them, four pairs crashing down onto the roof over their heads, a little to the rear of where the card game had been going on, The sounds were pacing about, until they all climbed down onto the lower deck. Through this, Jak had done her best to brace the hatch, especially since no-one else was helping her, she used her knife and sawed through Tuscus' bunk, taking the boards out and placing them through the door latch. The sounds were trying to find a way in.

Jenaro was holding back as far as he could, behind everyone else, with his muttering quieted down into a chant running through his mind, but not verbalized any more. He thought they had all heard him, and he was embarrassed. He did not think he'd live, so he kept quiet, not really because he was worried what they thought of him, they were dying soon too, but more because he didn't want to die that way. He wanted to die asleep, surrounded by apprentices and his spouse, all of which ideally would not mind that he had given away all his belongings to the church.

The hatch bulged in, and the board started to splinter, it pulsed again, and again, a heartbeat on the wood that burst inward and hurt his eyes with the sudden daylight (and the sight of a bright blue Tuscus, which he ignored, why, he doesn't know why, maybe it is because it was in the periphery of his mind). A head, black in the light from behind it, was coming through, a long sharp blade of shiny, treated bone glinting with a white reflection of the sun in its hand. The head was sharply defined - it had no hair, completely bald everywhere and a light, annoying hum that just nagged at the back of his ears, like a distant high-pitched song, sped faster than any song could be sung.

The myrmidon fell down in the hatch, half blocking it, Jak pulled her dagger from its throat, her hand was trapped under its head. The creature then reared back and her knife fell from the hole in its neck, releasing her hand. The hole gaped wide open, a second mouth, vomiting blood and air, and he saw that its face was blank, the three eyes were still twitching from side to side, the deep brown and green mottled skin was paling to a gray. Then, two hands grabbed either side, two more grabbed the shoulders, and one pulled on the head, its ring finger gripping right above the high central eye, and the last hand tugged at the chest, between the ribs. When it was almost pulled all the way back and through the hatch by those huge hands, he saw that it was sexless, smooth where he should have seen genitalia. The body was thrown aside, and he saw two more, standing on either side of the hatch, and a third behind them. The eldest apprentice tried to run out into them, his face flushed, tears running down from wide eyes, his hands tight and pale around stick he took from under his bed, but Jak pulled him back, and punched him hard in the gut, and he sat down behind her, his eyes squeezed closed.

The next myrmidon climbed in through the door and this time, again, Jak stabbed at him, the dagger now red with both creatures' blood as this one too collapsed. And the hum, the hum which had been growing louder, it intensified its pitch, and the two remaining outside did not drag the body back, but shoved it forward, until it blocked the entrance entirely, except where their hands gripped the wood and pulled. The wood groaned, a loud, slow rip under the high ripple of sound that seemed to come from the two left. Jen moved forward, and though Jak pushed him back, he could not see anything or feel her hands. He stood next to the wall, and he was muttering prayers, down to his gut reactions and the training of seminary finally breaking through his panic or coming out because of it, when his reserve could no longer hold it in check. He hit the knuckles pulling on the wood again and again and they started to bleed, as did Jen's hands, but he didn't notice, his skin was ripped off by the wood he hit against, but the knuckles kept on pulling, and the wood broke out.

The corpse was grabbed and thrown out, and the two tri-eyed beasts (Jen doubted their intelligence, perhaps so he could not think of them as human) started to come in the cabin and again Jak's dagger became bloody, and Jenaro, he jumped forward and bit the neck exposed as its owner climbed through the hole. The creature beat at him, but Jenaro bit hard and ripped off its skin and went through the tendons. The taste of salt and iron filled his mouth, blood sputtered out through his cheeks, down his jawline. Then Jak's dagger hit again, and the blood stopped coming as much and the body went slack, the weight pulled the throat out of Jenaro's clenched teeth, leaving flesh in his jowls.

Tuscus sat in the back, and he watched this, and shook back and forth on his legs, and he could not see this priest as the boy whose hands he grabbed so long ago. The body fell into the cabin all the way, and Jenaro opened his mouth and let the flesh fall out, pushing it out with his tongue and he shook, cold blood in his hands. He just started again to think, and he did not want to. With his sleeve, he wiped his mouth again and again and again, harder and harder and harder, until his mouth started to bleed and he couldn't tell what blood was his and what blood was from the dead thing's throat.

Then, the thump-thump-thumps stopped, and Tuscus sat still, nothing moving in the silence filling the small barge's crew quarters, with the bodies lying in the hatch, their hands reaching forward, another two outside the cabin, their blood trail leading there. Jak was first out of the cabin, her dagger in hand, and when no one shot her, Jen and the apprentice followed slowly. Jen turned one of the bodies over on the deck, grunting as he did so, and he ran his hands over its skin, his eyes almost closed, breathing lightly through his lips. He couldn't think of a prayer, though he knew one was appropriate (actually, several were, from "Thank you for allowing me to live and serve you," or the more traditional "Please, Sailor, let them have something I can sell off") and for once he didn't mind this. He was glad to be calm enough that he could nearly look at these people who had attacked with only his heart moving so quick and his hands steady as they, or because they, pressed into the man's body, leaving pale trails as he glided them over its skin, the blood drying on his mouth and his lips cracking.

Jak let out her husband and the other deck hand and apprentice from the hold, she hugged her husband, briefly and quietly, and they took the bodies and rolled them off the deck. The bodies fell into the water and did not float very well. The current dragged them down where they bounced against the rocks until the bones were broken and skin ripped open, sweeping too fast past the fish until they lodged in rocks against the bottom of the river's shore to decomposed slowly, the fish only able to nibble on them, and they polluted the water around them for several months. Jen took the swords left behind by the corpses, even though they were too large, almost, for anyone on the boat to use with any ability and the bone blades, treated though they had been, were close to being shattered from obvious years of use. He then began to pluck the arrows from the hull and cabin.

Tuscus followed them out of the door and began to help, he had seen these creatures before, he knew, but he couldn't tell anyone that, how could he tell them that? Would he say "Well, they rescued me when I was fleeing the Sailor's Church" or "I worked with them when I was training to be an assassin"? He had seen them before, with Jen, when he was thirteen, he just did not want to remember, as they fought off the templars, defending his home, and he had camped with them for a month as he walked, avoiding the main rivers, through the newly Theocratic territory until they reached the border, but he couldn't share this, and, like most of that trip, he didn't want to think of it.

The apprentices climbed down into the water, looking

along the hull near the waterline, making sure it hadn't been breached. It was intact, but they didn't know then, and, more importantly, it gave them something to concentrate on. Tuscus walked to Jak and sat next to her while she was pulling the bolts out of the side of the cabin.

"We need to get moving," Tuscus said.

She continued to pull on the bolts. Jen had counted twenty-seven in all. The grouping was very tight, almost touching each other, the wood they had hit was cracking and splintering, the scarring nearly all the way through in a few places, and she was yanking on her fourth bolt.

"We need to get moving," Tuscus repeated, "I don't want to be late." He thought, if he showed up on time, and this was reported, maybe he could kill the man he had to deliver the message to. Maybe he could make it look like an accident, or, if he had enough time after he got there, he could frame the receiver as being disloyal, a Theocratic stooge, and then he would be a hero for exposing a traitor twice over. Then no one would ever know that the envelope had been lost, all that would be known is that he was punctual, and that could hardly be bad, could it?

Again, she said nothing to him. Again, she pointedly yanked out a bolt and refused to look at him.

"Please, we really need to move. I'll lose money. You'll lose money." He knew that this would work on her.

She turned to him. "You really think I want to stay here? You really think I want them to come back? I don't know why they didn't continue to attack. I don't want to know why."

"Maybe they had gotten what they want?" and as he said

it, he knew what it was they had been after. "Have you seen Fennish's body?"

"No. He wasn't ours to look after, anyway. We won't have to worry about him getting in the way. You did hire him. Why? He never did anything but sit and look at me. I think, I think he just saw me as meat. I think he would have eaten me, given the chance."

And then Tuscus knew that they had gotten what they were after. Fennish must have taken the letter, Fennish, who was dead and whose body was with these creatures that had to have come from the Council and they must have been a test, he had to find them and take the letter back, maybe he could talk to them.

XXIII

The Animate Corpse

Fennish drifted down the river, under one of the corpses. His blood mingled with the other creatures', he kept his mouth and nose in the crook of the thing's arm, and he held onto it where its waist went under the water. His skin shuffled from gray-blue to blue-gray, his blood mixed with the things' blood in a pool that floated ahead of them downstream. He slowly guided it to the shore, and used the time to recuperate. By the time the myrmidon's corpse had moored itself under the tree roots at the edge of the river, the roots reaching out, grabbing for the corpse, the teeth of the things digging into the corpse, drawing it further up into the nest of roots where it was added to the rest of the waste that it had been collecting over the years, he had stopped bleeding and was almost fully healed.

He heaved himself out of the water and looked out over

the river. The barge had moored itself to the opposite shore (he was quietly thankful) and he watched his crewmates scramble about over the deck, obviously yelling at each other. He could only tell from their gestures, it was too far for him to hear them or read their lips. He checked the letter, and it was still intact. It was curiously not wet at all. He was monstrously hungry. Healing that quickly always made him so. He reached under the tree and pulled the corpse, already starting to bloat as the tree's digestive cells went to work, reducing it to consumable matter, from under the roots, ripped open an arm with his fingernails, closing his mouth, nose and eyes quickly to avoid the spores which spewed out, and started eating.

While he sat there, he opened the envelope, no longer concerned with keeping it pristine. In it, he found a single sheet of paper. As he ate, he read it. It was a letter of confirmation, telling the recipient that their budget request had been received. He folded the letter up and returned it to the envelope.

He rested, chewing, gradually feeling better, as the sun went down, and he saw two figures, the priest and the punk, leave the boat and start through the forest in the direction that they had been shot at from.

XXIV

Two Boys Go Romping in the Forest

Tuscus was walking with Jen through the forest. He had lost the argument with Jak on who was to search for their ambushers, but he had planned to. He thought that, as much as a stretch as it was, that they had taken his letter. Maybe they had found it on the boat, but then why would CouncilAd soldiers attack, and what they were doing here, in the open, that made no sense to him. The whole task was futile, he thought, but at least he was alone with Jen for the first time since they had left the nursery.

There was so much he wanted to say to the man, but he did not know if the priest walking in front of him was the same person he had left. He was sure Jen resented him for it. If Jen was not the same, how had he changed? He had been avoiding him on the barge, he knew Jen's job was to spy on him, he knew that he was the enemy. How could he think of this man, who he still saw in his mind as the boy who would tell him stories into the night, quietly, in their bunks next to each other, as they held hands until the needles descended into their arms and they went to sleep, their arms hanging limp off the edge of the bed, a red imprint on the underside of the upper arm, how could he think of this man as someone he should mistrust? How could he see him as someone he should spy on, as someone he should ruin? He had run away from him, the more he thought about it.

The autark who had set himself over Tuscus' ministry had made very clear to its subordinates, who had, in turn, done so to their trainees, such as Tuscus, that no one was to be taught to hate their enemies, as that was an inefficient use of their emotional energy, but that, instead, they should respect them and understand them. Tuscus, later, would come to realize that the reason his first mission was the one it was because they knew that Jen would be there, watching over him. No one had ever accused his masters of being incompetent.

He wanted to reach out to touch Jen's hand, to hold it tight in his, the way he would have at a younger age, but he wondered. Did the man have a lover, did he call the relationship that they had had puppy love, was he already married, did he have a husband waiting for him back at the seminary? He could only watch him from behind as they walked together through the forest, and he picked his way through with the same motions he remembered, a little more refined, a little more careful than he remembered, but not much more, not much different, the walk was still the way he had known it.

Tuscus wanted to just grab the man and hold him tight,

feel his body (just a little taller, so his chin would have to reach up to rest on his shoulder, but not too much so, just enough that he would feel protected) and the arms two tight arcs under his armpits, lifting him up a small amount. But he just walked behind and watched and, not knowing what to say, though maybe he hadn't argued with Jak as hard as he might have to get himself alone with the priest, and he kept quiet.

The priest was walking through the woods, and he could not see well enough. The merchant, who had begged him to come with him for company, though it was his job, and Jen would follow the man wherever he went because it was what he had to do, so he told himself, walked behind him, so quiet he forgot he was there. And the forest, he had always heard of forests being full of life, and they were, but he had always pictured insects everywhere, eating nuts and each other, chattering and running about, but he saw no movement in the waning light as Nod and Cain set (it was near the end of the week, and Cain was close to the sun, the next day would start with an eclipse) and the stars tried and failed to make their way through the canopy. The life of the forest was all tree and brush, and he could barely see them as he picked his way between their hanging roots. He was careful, or at least as well as he could be, to avoid the sharper roots, the ones he had been warned about by friends of his who went camping. He wished he had gone along with them once or twice, now. He walked further and further from the river, in what he hoped was a straight line. By the time he couldn't see in the dark night (or was it just the thick canopy as the trees fought each other leaf and root for the light, feeding off each other and straining to block the others out?) he couldn't smell the river or anything except the fecundity and fetidness of the forest.

Though it was dark, Jen saw a light ahead, a blue-green glow through the trees, and as he walked in the direction the arrows had come from, with Tuscus at his side. The trees grew blacker and blacker, until they were only outlines in the middle of the glow, and he could not, did not see anything but the light. He hit tree after tree, kicked their roots, shuffled and strode towards the light, and he couldn't resist it, it was the only source of direction he had. He had forgotten the boat, he didn't know why he was here, he forgot all about the arrows that had been shot at him, that he could never really have done anything about anyway. Tuscus was grabbing his shirt, in part because he didn't want to lose Jen, in part because some part of him, that bit deep down which was scared of the light, did not want to let Jen know that he could see clearly through the light. It was a cold light, the sources out in the open and sucking in the heat, he could almost feel it.

Then, as though the world itself had ended, the trees he bumped into were no longer in front of him, but beside him. In front of him (as his eyes adjusted to the light, but Tuscus' already had, and he had seen this all along, the contrast not hurting him at all) was a mud and stick tower, with no roof, two stories tall, like carefully shaped kindling, reinforced with mud, then kicked hard. Two other lumps were in sight, on either side to some distance, at the edge of the forest. Behind them, seeming in the center of the arc the three made, there sat a pile of stone that once had been very sturdy. He could see that, but then, any stone building looked sturdy to Jen, in great part because the only ones he'd seen in the past had been bunkers and cathedrals moored to the lake floors. In fact, the building before him was close to falling down, held up more by the vines growing through the cracks in the stone than by the mortar.

But what really held his interest, what he was focusing on, with the other buildings no more than nagging distraction, was the source of the light in front of him. At first it seemed to be a column, but as his eyes adjusted, he saw that the light was coming (quite softly really, in the day, he never would have noticed it, but on the night with the stars invisible and Cain gone from the sky, it was all-encompassing) from a disc suspended in the air between two smooth blocks, the top block also floating. He thought the blocks were bone, but they were far too big, and they were too smooth to be stone, how he could see them through the light coming from the disc was something else he couldn't quite figure out not that he thought about it. They were glowing in their own right, but softer still. The disc drew his eyes in to look at them solely, and he stood still at the edge of the forest, one foot slightly raised and he did not move, did not think to move, and his stillness was complete.

Tuscus saw the same blocks, the same disc, he saw them well before Jen did, while they were deep in the forest. He held onto Jen's arm, lightly, the first two fingers and his thumb wrapping about Jen's forearm, and he looked out into the clearing. He saw movement in the towers, movement which was drawing up taller on their roofs. He did not move, his color (Jen was not watching, he hoped) shifted into a deep green, the color he hoped the woods were. He was wrong, he would have stood out against the brown and red that was localized to this clearing, but it was dark enough that no one could have told the difference, the light from the discs was too coherent to show any color other than a single shade of blue. Jen could not turn his head to look back at Tuscus, he did not feel Tuscus' hand on his arm, he just saw the light. The creatures in the tower were growing taller and taller, then stopped growing, the tower tops stayed static for a moment. Then, with his mind speeding and seeing things happen slower than they were, three arrows, one from each tower, were arcing toward them, and he tried to pull on Jen, but the priest would not move, and he stood still, the arrows coming towards them, and he could not decide whether to run, to move in front of Jen, or to stay still, and then he had no time to chose, for the arrows were in the ground before him, a tight cluster, and another flight was in the air, landing with the others, then a third, with nine arrows making a triangle of triangles.

Even so, Jen walked slowly into the circle of the clearing, toward the disc floating and its light. He felt colder and colder the closer he came to it, and a few steps away, he saw his breath for the first time in his life. He watched it obscure the disc briefly, the mist rising out of his body. He reached forward as he walked to it, but he became cold, too cold, and his fingers burned with pain, and then his arm and then his chest, and the air he couldn't breathe. He saw ice crystals collecting on the ground near the disc, he saw dead animals like statues close to the slab that the disc floated over, he saw air dripping from it, a clear liquid like water, but boiling where it hit the ground.

He could not move from it, his body wasn't doing what

he wanted it to, and Tuscus reached for him. Walking behind the priest, Tuscus could see these things before Jen could, and he did not see the disc as brightness. In his night vision, while Jen and the archers (he knew that was what they were) showed as bright spots in a gray landscape, this thing was a black pit hanging in the air, the air which normally was a slightly darker gray than the land around it, the air which as bright as the sun by comparison. Tuscus reached for Jen and pulled him back from the disc, and the priest felt his arm then his fingers grow from numbness to incredible pain creeping from his skin, and then warmth.

Tuscus guided the priest into the heap of stone. He thought, so expensive it was. What could be in it? All he knew was that it was the brightest thing in his sight, next to the archers and Jen. The grass, moss, and shrubbery had been burnt away. He knew that the clearing wasn't natural. The burn had left only a carbon-black ring of ashes that they walked through, leaving their footprints in the ankle-deep powder, following and trying to get Jen to do so as well, footsteps already laid down. The door, which was also stone and seemed extravagant, could have stopped a horde when it was intact, so long ago. As Tuscus guided Jen over it, he still had to climb almost half again his height. All the while, he dragged Jen along with him as the priest left his eyes back to the discs. But then they crested the door, and Tuscus saw the something that ate away at his vision, a hole in his sight that ate up everything else he could possibly have seen.

Jen's eyes snapped forward, and he looked, this time without the distraction of the discs. The inside of the building was lit with the same glow, not as bright, but close, as the discs that lit up the clearing, and the glow was coming from a clear slab in the exact center of the room. On either side of him, he saw tapestries, lit up by the glow, and they had faded into thick rags, hanging from the walls, held up by rods in jagged concrete. Next to the tapestries, there were two doors, one on either side of the rubble they had climbed over, and they were made of rough wood, untreated and barely holding together. In front of the entrance, across the room, there was a throne (or so it seemed, as it sat by itself, on a dais made of dried mud). The throne that was also made of rough wood, just a seat of a board on top of four sturdy branches supporting it. Behind the throne was also a tapestry, and this one had a pattern visible even in the light of the glow, though it was black. It was smeared about on the cloth, smeared about in such a way, such a haphazard manner, that it seemed to draw him in, as he tried to find a rhythm or a image, but he was unable to do so.

As his eyes focused, he saw the slab clearer and clearer, and he saw tubes, coils clustered around the base and top, veins and tendons bulging underneath and stretching up to the ceiling, some as thick around as his arm to others skinny enough to be a mere fuzz in his eyes. The block was transparent, save for the glow, but that was also clear. In it, he saw, at first, a human figure shorter and stockier than a normal man. If the figure had been standing, it would not have reached Jen's chin, though it was almost half again as thick as the priest.

As he focused further, mentally removing the tubes leading to the block that obscured his sight, he saw the figure was more like a sketch of a human, with the edges ill-defined, a large flattened orb where the head was, a thick rope descending down from the orb, and that rope branching into four clusters that grew out from it and formed the limbs, and then, as he saw the definition, so very fine and so thick, in the hands and the eyes resting underneath the orb. The eyes were light blue, almost white, a color he had not seen before in anyone's eyes. He remembered seeing something like this before, seeing it in seminary, and he remembered his anatomy from his early days when he had first entered school. He saw this thing in the block and he knew that this was a nervous system, and he looked at the eyes, but they could not have blinked.

Then, he heard a noise behind him, and he looked about. Tuscus had disappeared, and saw the doors ajar, and ran to them. He closed the door behind him. The room smelled of sewage, but he was too scared to notice. He looked through the many cracks in it to see three of the three-eyed creatures walking into the throne room, and then leaving through the other door, the one across from him. When they closed the far door, he turned to see where he was, and he saw crates and crates, smelling them now, and he saw, in the dim light from the cracks, shapes scurrying amidst them. He walked carefully away from the door and tried to find a crate to hide behind, but they were firm against the walls. The walls were stone and cold and smooth and wet, the crates also smooth, but soft, with the bone nails sticking out and catching his fingers as he ran his hands over them, pricking him when he was not careful. He was not strong enough to move them, but he felt his way along the crates, trying still, until he came to a door. Behind it he heard nothing, even when he pressed his ear up to it, so close he could feel bugs crawling through it, dining on the wood, and then he opened the it. He could not see for the bright light that burned his eyes after the dim, a light so bright it seemed to be day.

As his eyes adjusted to the light, he saw a body in among the crates, lying in a bed of damp and musty leaves, with dead skin flakes around it. There was a bucket, with the contents spilled about. The body itself looked like a fetus, with a huge head and chest almost the size of a normal person's and small arms and legs, each not reaching half the length of the torso. Like the creatures outside, it was sexless. Though it was lying on its back, its legs were clenched in a circle around air. Its head was devoid of eyes, though in the place of ears were large membranes that covered either side of its head. As he looked closer, Jen saw that its throat had the same membranous covering, standing out a bit, and then it talked and he heard a buzz high above its voice, the same buzz he had heard from those creatures that were trying to break into the barge. He watched the membranes flutter, and he did not hear what it said. It spoke louder and then he heard the voice, more of a soft hum in his head, right in the back above his neck, just where his spine met his skull.

Though he did not understand what it said, he took the thing in his arms. It was soft, there were no bones in it at all, pure cartilage. It was top heavy but light enough for him to carry, and its skin was dry on top, but its back was moist, and he didn't want to think about how that could be. The bed of leaves it had been lying in was brown, crumbly, and obviously wet. His arm stuck to the creature when he shifted it around to get a better grip. Then it screamed, not so Jen would notice, though he felt a wave of nausea that coursed through his bowels. He held it next to his head, where the buzzing of the membrane felt nice on his cheek, then he raised it onto his shoulders. Its legs snapped about his neck, and the little arms grabbed his hair tight in their fists, they pulled and hurt, but he let it, he moved his head carefully where there was a tug on his hair, and it didn't hurt anymore.

When Tuscus first heard the noise, he tugged at the priest, but Jen was too deep staring into the hole in Tuscus' vision. He pulled again on his arm, but Jen did not notice at all. The noises came closer and closer, and he could not wait any longer, he did not want to die, so he ran through the door to his right, one that he saw no life behind. The other was so full of life it glowed, pulsed in his mind. There, he found a room of crates, the crates intact and well kept, their tops pried off, only a little warmer than the stone, and their contents were uniform to his sight. He reached a hand in, and felt cloth wrapped around a hard, long object. He unwrapped it, and felt along it again, but he cut himself. He grabbed the cloth, and wrapped it again around the object, and pulled it out, and felt through the cloth more carefully, and he felt that the thing was a sword, only as long as his forearm, but very, very sharp. He grasped the hilt tight with his unhurt hand (unfortunately, he had reached in with his right hand, the hand he favored) and took the cloth, hoping it was clean because he knew his clothes weren't anymore. He tied it tighter and tighter around his hand, until he felt his circulation was cut off, then he loosened it a little, just as he had been taught. He wished he had something to eat, and he knew that he would be starving by the time he finished healing.

But then Tuscus heard behind him the door open. He turned and saw three shapes through the wall, and he ran down the corridor, bruising his legs on the boxes as he bounced back and forth, the sword in his left hand smacking into them, jarring his arm, and he ran into a door at the end of the hall. He saw a figure behind it, but he did not acknowledge it, for it was still, and prone, and the three things behind him were tall, and fast, and coming closer.

The door fell open, and in the room, unlit, there lay a huge man on a bed, a long, thick sword by his side, his hand resting near it, with a chest at the base of the bed. Both the chest and the bed were well-made, both were of wood that was smooth and heavy to his eyes, and the bed itself was draped in blanket after blanket, all thick and soft. The man was naked and large, his skin gleamed in Tuscus' vision, his hair was long and fell around his head like water spilling over from a fountain. His arms and legs were strong, his stomach was a little swollen, but not much so. His toes were spread, holding the sheets, and his right hand was clasping his left arm tight. But then, the man only was incidental to Tuscus, once he focused again on the long sword lying beside him. It looked different than he had ever seen. It was colder, he reached his hand out to it, he breathed on it, and he saw that it was metal, steel, and he had never seen such a weapon, one made solely of metal, even the hilt, and his reaching hand touched it. His arm was jolted back, he was flung by the huge arc of electricity that coursed from the sword through his body, and, before he lost consciousness, he saw the man on the bed, his hair flowing down, rise up, and look at him with eyes, eyes that when they focused were clearly mad.

XXV

Back at the Boat

Jak sat on top of the deck, looking at the sky, waiting for the sun to rise. The eclipse would happen less than an hour after sunrise, and she woke up early for it every week. She had seen it without fail for twenty years, and she loved the sight still. She loved the way the sun slowly was eaten by Cain as they both rose together in the sky, the way the world went black for a moment when the sun was fully eclipsed, then your eyes adjusted, and the stars came out, and you could see Cain's other moons in the reflection of its light, yet the corona broiled about Cain, not bright enough to wash out the painting that the sky was, but strong enough to take away the bands of color that washed over Cain's surface and turn it into a black disc. She wondered frequently how the earlier ages had seen the sky. If the gods had not already existed, would they have been made out of this event, would Cain be the god of evil (or good) and the sun the god of good (or evil)? Would each of Cain's moons been a separate god, each growing and shrinking in power as the sun shifted about them? Or would the weekly eclipses just become such a part of life that they are automatically relegated to the position that they served to Jak, that of simple time keeping.

Her husband would try to watch with her, but more often than not, he could not stay awake long enough, and so he would end up passed out in her lap the way he was at that moment on the barge, and she would play with his hair. It was so short, like her own, and she loved the way it sprung against her hand when she ran her hands over it, even though, if he had been awake, he would have complained, but asleep, he just rubbed his face stronger into her thigh. She did not think of the two boys in the woods who were gone almost ten hours by then, she did not think of the repairs that the barge still needed, though not much more needed to be done, just cleaning up and testing the motor, she did not think of Fennish, standing on the edge of the boat, as he was shot through again and again with the bolts and fell into the water.

She would only think of the rising sun and the rising planet which was already up a ways, and so much slower, the river water passing beneath them, the trees encroaching slowly upon the river, leaning over it, framing it, and she saw the sun rise fully over the forest, with its light washing through the leaves (fought for so vigorously that some light made it through the dead spaces) and splashed into the river, rippling with it, and then the planet Cain biting into the disk of the sun Nod, barely visible against the glare, but she kept her eyes on Cain, she could see the bands of clouds at the upper edge, and she bent over and kissed her husband's hair, with the feel of it between her lips, in her teeth, she straightened back up and watched the week begin.

XXVI

Another Educational Interlude

In the earliest days of human habitation, after the rocks fell and most gods died, leaving the Ship alone, the nurseries became centers of power. Allegiance to the one who controlled the nursery meant that the peasant could be rewarded with livestock and crops, as well as assistance from people who were most likely born of that same nursery. The dukes (for that is what they called themselves) held tight to their power, and they handed down the secrets for caring for the incubators from generation to generation, soon breeding slaves whose sole purpose was to take care of the machines, using pure, slow, trial and error to find a human who could live in the underwater caves which were the most common places to put the nurseries. Those slaves, with their hypersensitive vision and ability to subsist on lichens and roots alone, were the beginning of the specialization that would spread through the planet. They were also the last innovation for some centuries, for they allowed the dukes to battle each other for more and more nurseries. Rarely would a duke could ever control more than three complexes, usually the soldiers they churned out from the incubators consumed too much food and land to allow for much further incorporation, and the few empires, for such they were called by those who pretended to themselves they controlled whole continents, would invariably fall with the death of the duke.

This was the world the Sailor was born into, one which had stagnated, not because of any concerted effort, but because the chaos prevented any developments from passing from one state to the other, from one generation to the next. The Sailor took this world and proved to it the most important law of any society, that profit and the potential for profit will destroy any allegiance. The Sailor proved this, for the nurseries were forgotten in favor of the apprentice of the garbage scow pilot, relegated there as the duke who spawned the Sailor did not deem the Sailor to be of any use.

That child could guarantee that those who pledged themselves to that first corporation would live better than the previous generations. When the first nursery was bought from under a duke who was in very dire straits, the corporation that would become the Sailor's church established itself as a going concern. The Sailor bought more and more, the corporation's ships passing from city to city, slowly exchanging badly needed goods for control in portions of the cities they visited. Eventually, dukes found themselves left with nothing of their duchies, the body of the nation taken from them through their need, held by people who they could not easily attack without risking revolt and starvation. They could breed new people still, at least those who were left with their nurseries could, which not all of them were.

But those people would be some years before they could be useful, and they could not be fed without the Sailor's food. It is impossible to breed for consumption if there are no resources to put into those being bred. And, as several of the more stubborn found out, while their cattle and grain was shipped exclusively through the Sailor who they had offended, humans were very poor food animals, too stringy and gristly, extremely infectious, with very little in the way of large edible portions. They even made bad sausage.

These dukes fled their lands, leaving them to the corporation, not willing to deal with the Sailor. Others, recognizing that they could, in turn, make a profit and grow in power to an extent they could not have dreamed of, joined the corporation or founded rival companies, though these were few and far between, especially relative to the general populace. As in most societies, the aristocrats weren't as intelligent as they were arrogant. In exile, the fled dukes borrowed and pleaded, leaving them still further in debt, for armies they led against the Sailor, only to find themselves defeated, not by any direct conflict, but by lack of food, lack of weapons, and rampant desertions.

So, when the Sailor was dying of old age, one of the few rulers to do so in the history of the planet then and since, the Ship recognized the shift the Sailor had caused, and it knew that the result of the collapse of the Sailor's corporation would be a regression back to the anarchy of warlords, and it summoned the Sailor up to the itself. A coffin fell to the water and the Sailor was placed into it. They rose together into the sky, and when it returned, the Sailor was no longer human, but a god, like the Ship. The Sailor appointed a patriarch, the one who had been its lover, and then had itself buried under the ground in the catacombs formed by water flowing under the island, left behind when the same was dammed away, beneath the headquarters of the corporation. The patriarch transformed the corporation into a church based on the life of the Sailor, and the Church was born.

Unfortunately for some, the Sailor was an active deity and had no qualms about correcting the doctrines made in its name. For example, early on it insisted on being called an it. Gender is inappropriate for a god, it would always argue, for a god does not reproduce sexually and any choice of gender would imply a preference. The corpus of the Sailor had no sex physically, and it had been very careful to expunge all references to its sex over the millennia, as it felt it was originally unfairly privileged or discriminated against. No one could ever get a straight answer, even from a god as clear spoken as the Sailor, but they did not press the issue, as pressuring a god is not the most healthy or respectful of activities.

Those who saw the Sailor, deep in the ground, were in fact only seeing what had since become known as its avatars, genderless, naked, tall, and athletic, with purple-black skin and straight, long red hair, a trait that had only existed in one equatorial province, of which the duke of the province had exterminated all those with similar traits as his last act to defy the oncoming armies of the Sailor, traits not since resurrected out of deference to the sailor. Those avatars would never give away the actual location of the god, at least no more specifically than somewhere under the city, which had been known publicly anyway by the power the priesthood exerted on reality in the holy city.

Eventually, the other dukes who still retained their duchies united against the Sailor's Church. They each abrogated some of their power into a council of autarks. Each duchy became more specialized, by necessity, as it competed with the all-consuming Theocracy. With proper nudges by the Ship (which recognized early on that the Sailor's Church would fall into stagnant tyranny worse than warlords without competition), the council of autarks became an oligarchy of administrators and their subjects were bred into functional castes, organs in the great body of the state.

As the Church waxed and waned and waxed again under pressure of the human hive of the Ducal Council, the Sailor remained the only constant, an eternal and necessary point of contention.

XXVII

The Boys Wake Up

When Tuscus woke up, he was hungry, so hungry, and his skin was raw on his clothes, the palms of his hands were electric. He could feel his skin growing back over them. He was before the hole in his vision, staring up at it, and the man, the large man, still naked, holding the metal sword lightly in his left hand and a bone sword in his right, was standing in front of the hole. The bone sword's point was resting on his body, he noticed, as he woke up further, and it was warm, the temperature of his skin, if not warmer. He could see the entrance behind both the hole and the man, and, over the rubble, light poured in from the outside, light dulled by mist, but light nonetheless. Arranged in an arc around him, the hole, and the man were the tall three-eyed things. He noticed Jen in their midst, carrying a head on top of his own, or so it looked to him, lying on the floor. Jen was arguing with the man.

"Let him go."

"No," said the man, in a high-pitched voice, one that was obviously falsetto, it tried to rumble from beneath his stomach, but the man with the swords would not let it.

"We are leaving. You can't keep us here any longer."

"You will stay, or I shall curse you. You will not live out the week."

"We could kill you now."

"You can not. My god protects me well."

"Only if you stay there. You must leave your god to eat and drink. And then we will kill you. Let him go, and we won't. We'll just take everything with us, and we'll leave you with your god, just the way we found you."

"No. You will stay. The god commands it."

Tuscus eyes readjusted to the daylight, and the hole was no longer a hole in his vision, but the nervous system Jen had seen earlier. The eyes were staring directly at the head that the priest was carrying. The man still faced Tuscus, and the sword still pricked his skin.

"Ah well," Jen said. And then, from all sides, bolts shot out toward the man, and they were all reaching for his head, but they all smacked into the floor or ceiling before they reached him, or they would hit his skin and shatter. Again the bolts flew, with the same result.

"I will kill the boy," the man said, pressing the sword into Tuscus' skin, but again the bolts flew, this time for the tubing above and below the god, and the man raised the metal and bone swords, too quick to see, and he slapped them from the air, but he could not get them all. The bolts that did not miss sliced open the tubes, and gas poured out, covering the floor, with rolling, cold, white clouds. Tuscus scampered back quickly, and bumped against the throne. There was no food there, but he grabbed some of the cushion, ripped it off, and stuffed it in his mouth, and his mouth was kept busy gnawing at it.

The creatures and Jen were walking steadily out the door, and Tuscus ran to join them, past the man who was now facing his god on his knees, his hands working as fast as they could to hold together the tubes that had been severed, and staring into the lidless eyes as they stared back at him, his legs and hands already white and covered with frost. Tuscus climbed over the rubble in the doorway to see Jen hand the body that had rested on top of his head to one of the three-eyed creatures. He turned back to the inside of the structure and watched through his so strong hunger as the god shattered, skewering the man and bursting him into a white mist.

Tuscus was dragged back, and he saw the roof buckle and fall in, the walls imploding, the rubble that they climbed over rush inwards toward where the god had been, and the wind dragged at him, but the hands grabbing him were strong enough to keep him from following it. The cushion was sucked from his mouth, as was his breath. When the rush of wind stopped, the roof fully collapsed, the hands let go of him, and he climbed back into the building. The inner walls were collected were the god had stood, but there, on top of it, as it if it had wormed its way up, was the nervous system, in a lump. It was clean and steaming cold, but that didn't stop Tuscus, and he ran to the mass of flesh and ate it right there as the myrmidons and Jen, who was looking very dazed and very disgusted, followed him in.

With his stomach sated, his mind returned to the reason he had left the barge and he thought of the letter. His letter was lost now for good. He knew these folk could not have had it, would not have taken it, even if it had been on the barge in the first place. But could he possibly fake the letter? What would have been in it, he did not know, but maybe he could extrapolate it. He thought for a while, picking his teeth with his tongue, catching the bits of the god that had snagged themselves in the cracks of his teeth. Then he saw the crates of food, and he saw the crates of weapons. The food crates had shattered, but then, they had been undermined by the wildlife and eaten by the myrmidons. He called Jenaro over. Jen hesitated, and Tuscus called him again, and he knew what he wanted, he knew what he needed to do for the first time since he left training.

"Brother!"

"Yes?"

"You were talking for these people before, weren't you?" Tuscus asked.

Jen hesitated. "Yes, but..."

"Can you still do so?"

"Maybe. I don't want to, though. Not the same way."

"How do you feel about making some money from this little side trip?"

The priest groaned, and started to turn way, then turned back to him and said "I suppose so."

"You see those crates over there?" Tuscus pointed to the weapons. "What would you say about selling them?"

"I don't know if they would get much."

"They didn't cost us anything. They don't have to pull in too much money. It's all profit."

"Who would buy?"

"The miners, the smelters, the scrubbers, anyone. There's always a market for weapons. No matter where you go, someone's always ready to buy. I'm sure I can find a distributor."

"But how would we get them to the barge?" Jen did not want to have any part in selling a dead god's treasure. He knew it would be cursed, though he had never been taught so. In fact, had he been paying attention, he had been taught that selling anything would remove any curse because the transaction sanctified it. He could have guessed that if he thought for a minute about the Church's history, but history was not where his mind was. At that moment, it made sense to him not to disturb anything that the eaten god had touched.

"You can talk to them, right? Convince them they owe us something"

"How would I do that? I'm not talking to them again, not like that." Jen shuddered at the idea. After having the fetus-creature on his back, he knew what it was like to be soulless.

"I don't care how, just convince them, these people look strong, they can carry the crates back, easy."

Jen sputtered.

"Hey!" Tuscus called out, "Hey! Three-eyes!" He turned back to Jen. "Which one is their leader?"

"They don't really have a leader. Well, maybe the small one."

"Hey!" Tuscus called again, addressing the creature

holding the fetus-creature on its shoulders, "Would you help us?"

"Do what?" it asked, the first sound Tuscus had heard from these things. Its voice was hoarse, unused, cracking through the octaves, hitting three extra notes in the sound of the word.

"Take these crates," he gestured to the ones filled with weapons "to our boat."

"Why?"

"Why?" Tuscus whispered to Jen.

"I don't know. Wait, wait, I'm not helping you."

"C'mon, anything. It's your divine duty, you know."

Jen sighed. "Tell them I rescued the head. That's close enough to the truth."

"Thanks." Tuscus went up to the creature, as close as he could without having to crane his neck. "He saved you. He wants you to do it. You owe him. Pay him back."

"Is this what you want?" The thing addressed Jenaro. Jen shrugged, then nodded, facing away from it. "We do owe him. We will return the favor. This one." The other creatures slowly walked to the crates and began repackaging the ones that had been damaged when the building had collapsed.

"Smile, Brother, we're going to make some money!" He grinned at the priest. He knew that the Theocrats loved money, and he knew that Jen would like him more, the more money they made. And if he served his more pressing urges, so much the better.

"They'll take some time to finish. Let's poke around for anything else we can scavenge, eh?" He headed toward the cell where the fetus-creature had been held, but there was nothing there of interest, and nothing he could feign it in. He inspected what was left of the throne, and found it to be rough wood, poorly held together with glue that was stronger than the wood itself. He went to the bedroom, and hoped something there was enough to waken Jen's greed.

The bed and the trunk were intact, something that surprised him, with the ceiling fallen around it, in a cluster. They walked to the bed, under the eyes of the creatures, who were making no secret of it as one after the other, they watched them, their gazes flicking on them and off, but always one of them watching. The bed itself smelled of urine and spit, and they did not touch it, but the chest, its latch seemed broken, and Tuscus pried it open. In the trunk, he saw a carapace, the same type that he had fled when he was taken away from Nephi. This did not surprise him in the slightest. It didn't fit him, he was both pleased and disappointed to see, because he would have liked the protection, but then, he would not have wanted to fight over it with Jen, who could and would have to claim it as Church property. It also looked as if it might be dangerous, it was so old and worn, and it looked as if there might be hairline cracks in the thing. What did surprise him was when the pulled the shell out of the chest, and knocked it back a bit, and a burst of cool air rose up from under the chest. Tuscus dropped the armor in surprise.

XXVIII

Under the Temple

He shoved the chest all the way away from the bed, and beneath it, a spiral staircase descended, lit by a soft glow from the edges of the steps. It dropped far down, it seemed, though the steps blocked any real view that they might have had. They climbed down the steps, and they did so for long minutes in the quiet, not wanting to draw attention to themselves, and their feet on the steps made no noise. They sank in a bit, their feet were wrapped in the steps, though they didn't even notice that until they had passed several turns.

When Jenaro got to the bottom, he saw before him, lit by strings of small lights along the ground, metal, metal, and more metal. He could barely see, but the light was reflected in the way that only metal, polished metal, could. It made him forget the embarrassment he had felt in the throne room, when

Tuscus ate the dead god, and he looked with love in his eyes, both avarice and wonder in his mouth's gaping. Even Jenaro, when in the presence of this much wealth, could not resist. It struck deeper than everything else he had ever learned, down to the primal greed of all humans. The metal was clustered directly under where the god had been, it smelled, not of oil, a smell he associated with metal all his life, but odd and crisp, and he walked toward it.

Damn my luck again, Jen thought, in the middle of nowhere, buried deep in the woods, I find a fortune, and I can't just forget it, and I can't just give it away, I have to keep it. As he walked, following the lights that all led to the center, he knocked into something, and a rustle, dry, then a clatter, loud in the place, echoing until the walls swallowed it. He looked down to see a dust covered chair, out of which had fallen a skeleton, no, a corpse, the skin so dried that it pulled tight against the bones, the eyes now dust fallen from the sockets, and he jumped back from it.

After he caught his breath, he looked at the body again, and saw that the clothes were still brightly colored and intact. He looked where the body was sitting, and he saw the corpse was sitting at a bank of knobs and buttons. He looked closer at them, and, on the buttons, there were words in the old tongue, the language he hadn't learned enough of in seminary (he had passed the classes, but never went beyond the required) and they said to him "power" and "temperature" and numerous acronyms which he could not understand. He twisted the one named temperature, for it was cold in there, even though he was clothed, but nothing happened. He flipped all of the switches then, turned all the dials, and the one named power lit up the room.

And then the room smelled of burning dust, and he heard the great sounds of wind, and the place shone in his eyes. He and Tuscus started coughing as what little dust that didn't get burned was blown into their faces. Matrices of light grew from the tables and danced about the machinery in the center of the room, a mirror of the tubes and pipes and pumps that were clustered around the god upstairs, although all of them led through the ceiling of the chamber. In the matrix, the lattice of light, he read "God is dead, birthing demigods," and it flashed and cleared itself. Through the lattice, he saw it was not dusty at all near the machinery, unlike the rest of the room. The noise quieted to a hum.

The room started to get colder, and Jen took the clothes off the corpse and put them on. They were warm, very warm, and he was pleasantly hot fairly quickly. Behind him, Tuscus did the same. In his pockets in the new clothing, he felt lumps, and pulled them out to see a number of trinkets, one of which was a steel knife (though it was very light, something Jen did not know, and not at all steel). He looked at the lattice of light before him, and saw in there a stream of text in the old tongue, a tongue never spoken, just read, and in that text, what he could read, and he read it out loud to Tuscus and more to himself, he saw a story.

XXIX

Diaries of Dead Gods

*S*yem City is dead. Those bastards dropped a rock on it and killed everyone. With the god's help we were able to save him and bring him to his other self here. They won't penetrate this temple, that's for sure. When we get the god reborn we will try to contact the new capital, wherever it is.

Part of me wonders why it took them so long to start a war and part of me wonders how they could start one so soon. We've barely gotten settled here. It's not as if we didn't fight enough on Arbor Vitae.

I have just been told by Mary that she can't get in touch with Arbor Scientae. In fact, she can't even see it. She knows where to look, too. I hope it's returning to Eden.

Mary said she saw a flash where Babel was supposed to be today. I ran outside to look, and I saw what she said was the tail end of a series of smaller flashes, though what I saw almost blinded me. The radio (which is useless) spewed static for as long as Babel was above the horizon.

Mary and the god and I talked about it, and after what happened to Babel yesterday and the lack of contact with Syem (or what is left of it), we think it is better to move everything into the underground temple. We will keep an antenna and picture-box on the surface.

We've been here for a week, and Mary is nice and so is the god, but I am going stir-crazy. Every time I start to go upstairs, the camera shows a burst of light and mushroom clouds and the radio fills with static. I'd go up even so, if the ground didn't shake so much. It gets very loud in here when it does. The walls move. I don't know if the god can take it, but Mary assures me that it was born for this sort of thing. She says that it's a sturdy and resourceful god.

The god is alive, and it is talking to the new capital. The first prayers came through today, and we are following them. We are to feed the god and raise it up to the ground so it can talk easier.

Mary said today that she couldn't hear the god's prayers. We asked the god about this, and it protested that she was wrong, and we should have faith in it?

I think the god is mad and Mary agrees. It keeps asking for more power and more prayers, and it is speaking of the outside world as empty of civilization. Neither of us can leave here until the war is over, that is for sure, but I cannot believe that we are all that's left. We might have to kill the god to fix its soul.

How stupid could I be? I am sitting here, and I can barely breathe, and I know it is because I was so dumb as to record on a god that I am planning to kill it. The doors won't open, the antenna is broken, and we are all dead now, and the god is up there and nothing I can do down here will save us.

"And the story ends," Jen said, and he turned from the matrix to see one of the taller, three-eyed creatures standing at the foot of the stairs. "We are ready," it said, and it walked up the stairs. Jen turned to look at the machinery one last time and shuddered, feeling a curse descend upon him. He hurried to follow him, Tuscus already on his way up, and neither thought anything of Fennish's short man-shaped ripple that brushed past them as they made their way to the boat.

XXX

The Boys Return to the Boat

Jak saw the priest and the merchant break through the woods, and wave to her from the shore. They jumped in the water and started wading toward her, and she stood on the barge's edge, waiting for them with the same patience she had had when they had entered the woods almost half a day earlier.

Then she saw the things, those things that had killed a member of her crew. Admittedly, he had been Fennish, who she hadn't met until recently and had hated immediately, but she had never wanted him dead. They were carrying crates, and the merchant was waving them toward the barge with a huge grin on his face. It was the first time that she had not seen him scared of his own shadow, and she wasn't sure she liked the change. The priest looked very resigned to her, and he did not seem to be happy. Both of them had different, much brighter clothes on, of a somewhat shiny material. The priest climbed up from the water, nodded at her, said "Don't worry, they won't hurt us," and went into the cabin. The merchant stopped before her at the base of the boat.

"Is there any room? Of course there is. These gentlefolk have to load these on, I'll pay the extra transport costs. Hell, I'll let you have a cut of the deal, if you like."

"I don't..." Jak started.

"You wouldn't believe what we found. If I could tell you, I would, but I can't. We'll just have to come back here on our way downriver. Then you'll see. I just can't do it justice." He started climbing into the barge. "You'd like it though. Anyone would. Just tell them where you want them to put the stuff. It can get wet, don't worry about that. Rain won't hurt it. Boy, am I tired. You wouldn't believe how exhausting the walk back was. Good night." And he also disappeared into the cabin.

She looked over the creatures, all shin-deep in water, all loaded down with the crates, and looking back to her. She just waved them closer and started them stacking the crates on the floor of the barge.

An hour later, they had disappeared back into the forest, and the barge was close to being swamped from the weight of the crates, and she had the deckhands up, doing their best to fix what little was left to be done by lying on the crates, squeezing past them, and standing in the water. In another hour, they were on their way up the river again. She fell asleep in the middle of the night, the last one awake, the little internal combustion engine chugging away quietly, the sound more muffled than normal behind the crates.

She tried to stay awake, really she did. She thought the creatures might attack again or something else would happen, maybe a fallen tree would scrape the bottom off the barge, but it was impossible to remain awake. Her eyes grew heavy. The rhythms of the motor were soothing. The sky was quiet and clouded, just a black canvas over the water which had nothing to reflect and so was just as black as the sky. The shadows of the trees passed her by, the ripple of the water around the barge was a light punctuation to the motor. The smell of the burning ethanol was now just background, as had become the smells of the river itself. She knew this part of the river, and she wanted to stay awake through it. She had never been past it at night before, and the day, though easy, was beautiful to her, though this night she could not see anything, no matter how hard she tried. She tried to stay away, but she couldn't, and before the depths of the night, she had sprawled out on top of the cabin, asleep.

Her husband woke her, and she saw and heard through clouded eyes, the ones she rubbed sand from, and dense ears that both magnified and dampened every sound. She saw and heard the waterfall, dropping down from the sky to land in a cloud of water, visible even this far away. The mountains were around her with sparse trees and almost devoid of life. She could see through the trees, sometimes as far as two, maybe three hundred yards. The mountain streams were running quick down into the river. The edge of Lake Sali rose higher than most buildings, the falls the only leak that allowed any of the great mass of the lake's water through. And it poured through, even as far downstream as she was, the current seemed fierce from the water from the falls. She could hear the thrumming of the rope pulling the boat, again a rhythm to match the engine's, steady and long and deep, like the river itself tried to be. She could smell the smoke from the mining town.

Then she could see the smoke, rising black and brown and gray from the smokestacks just breaching the horizon, the ash from the smelter as it burned through any impurities. And then the long buildings, made so extravagantly of steel, and the carts trundling between them on the rails that stretched from under the lake to the buildings, many of them on land. The tallest water-borne building, the old Council administrative center, was still being transformed into a church after over a decade of Theocratic priests, and next to it, the hospital, floating near the shore, and the great docks where the steel was loaded onto larger barges than hers. The priest and the merchant, up now and just getting out of the cabin, had never seen buildings near that size on land, and even Jak, who had been to this town more times than she could count, still found them to be odd on the eyes.

They drifted into the small lake the town sat in. The small lake was created to slow the water as it fell from the falls, the lake that, in its creation, led to the discovery of the iron ore under the lake. The barge drifted out of the current, to the docks. On the other side of the docks, she saw the worker's homes, some of the street arc-lamps still on, the men and women walking around turning them off, and the barge drifted up to the dock where a smiling woman awaited them.

XXXI

The Town of Semt

The town of Semt is one that was said to be very old. At the pool that the waterfall made, coming off of a crater lake, it was always a beautiful place, with the plants rising up in an inverse fall of their own, creeping high up the rock, near the top mere tendrils, but covering the waterfall completely in many places in a cage of vines. The more adventuresome of the town folk would climb those vines, they were thick and strong enough, and feel the spray from the waterfall under them, striking their bodies length ways in a hard mist. Even more daring would climb to the top and jump down into the pool, which was deep enough to cradle any who fell into it, if they hit near the fall itself. Others would jump along the vines, reaching and stopping themselves by grabbing on to the stray tendrils that arched into the air, abusing the occasional plant trying to catch the spray, almost pulling their arms out of their sockets in the process.

At the top of the fall was a lake, Lake Sali, a near perfect circle, marred only by the scar that opened to allow the waterfall. There was an island in the center of the place, a strange small peaked land, said to be inhabited by ghosts, and the inevitable camping ground of the curious. Over the millennia (for the town was really that old, the inhabitants said that to each other, but they had no idea how accurate they were when they told of the town being the oldest in the world at four millennia), a small hut had been built and maintained from the strangely permanent bones found on that island, the very bones that gave rise to the ghost stories. It was a hut without a thick roof, but it would keep the height of the rainy season off who ever was in it. At the edge of the lake, a boathouse watched over a raft made from the same strange bone. Both the hut and the raft were bound together with vines that had to be reinforced every season.

Down below the falls, around the pool, a single building had served as store, post office, newspaper, and government offices. There were no real industry and no nurseries, though the latter had been tried not long after the founding, but the mutations in the fetuses were almost as horrible as those conceived and carried naturally, and all were stillborn. The town had served as a retirement community for some times, as a refuge in others, a monastery for a good portion of the time to a dead religion (their god could not perform the miracles that others could, and so the monks and nuns gradually died out or lost their faith), a duke's summer home, and most recently, and most often, simply a place for those who wished to bow out of mainstream society but did not want to leave humanity altogether. The average age of the place had ranged from fifty to one hundred twenty, depending on the century, and the various houses, some on the same site for uncountable centuries, with interesting results for those who dig gardens, reflected this, a eclectic combination of ramps and high steps, rope ladders and dumbwaiters.

But the most significant aspect of the town, until recently, had been its anonymity. It had always been under the control of whoever controlled Nephi, down the river, and the duchy of Nephi had been one of the last incorporated into the great empires (first the Church, then the Council, then, most recently, the Church again). The region made a fine border state, and its annexing had only occurred as the region went bankrupt and was bought by a woman in search of a bishopric. The attempt failed, and the woman went broke on the venture.

There had been a good reason why Semt and Nephi had been steadily losing money. Even then, no one paid much attention to it except as a place where the cast offs and the unfavored were exiled by the Patriarch or Matriarch of the day. The Theocracy was only too happy to give the region up in the resolution of one of the many border wars with the Oligarchy, a deal which cost the Council diplomat his life. And so, Semt had been left alone for the majority of its history. At its very origins, this was different, but that story had been aggressively forgotten early on, in part due to the shame of losing its high place in the world.

But then, twenty years before Jen and Tuscus and Jak went up the river together, the Ducal Council, which still had Nephi at the time, finally sent someone to Semt to study the odd bones. It had taken so long because the Oligarchy was horribly efficient in everything it did. An oddly made hut and raft at the borderlands was hardly important, and hardly warranted the risk and cost of sending an anthropologist and materials scientist. But it did happen, at a time when the region was at relative peace, and a geologist (the best they could do) was free to look and bring back the artifacts.

The geologist found something no one had expected, something no one had seen for the four millennia that Semt had been a blip on a map. The geologist recognized the land almost immediately as a crater, a huge one, the result of a meteorite that had fallen long ago (four millennia, in fact, right at the time Semt went from being a metropolis to a collection of shacks) but it had remained undisturbed since then. And she knew what meteorites tended to be made of, but she took her core samples and found the most precious of metals there, the one that was most lacking on the planet, the one that usually existed only in red clay. Iron. Cold and shiny, it had not even yet oxidized in that first sample.

The town of Semt grew tenfold in the course of a year, and the mine was sunk and the smelting plants and mills were built, clearing up the fruit trees that had been growing there. Miners were bred and imported. Their eyeless heads with long noses, short legs, strong arms, and incredible endurance were seen everywhere in the mines. Lifters laid the tracks for the carts carrying the ore from building to building.

Years later, the younger generation were still alive and working, while the miners had long since died out only a few years after the Church took over. Iron and steel flowed out. The waterfall was harnessed for the electricity needed to produce the steel, and the mine under the lake grew. The region had become important again. The Church began moving quietly into Nephi, which was still the only route to Semt, and the Nephites (those very few with free will), called for the Sailor's Church to enter. And the rest rolled itself out.

No one ever seemed to notice that there was too much iron, too pure iron, for it to be simply the result of a meteorite. The geologist had predicted possibly five years worth of mining. But the mining had continued unabated for twenty years with no end in sight. War was not something deemed important enough for either the Oligarchy or Theocracy to stop or slow down of any business. They both knew what was of prime importance, after all. The miners, once the Church moved in and had standard humans (close enough) working the site, started competitions for the oddest rock formations or trinkets found under the lake. But still, the raft and the hut are used, mostly at night in the dry seasons when Cain is in the sky and the noise from the waterfall roars loud enough to block the round-the-clock work below.

XXXII

Agitator

After showing everyone else on the boat where to unload his original cargo (he kept the weapons on the boat until he felt he could unload them safely, ostensibly so he could decide whether he would sell them in bulk or piecemeal), Tuscus ran up to the woman who greeted them at the dock while everyone else was still busy tying the boat up. He looked over the woman and saw the tattoo he was told to look for, and he saw the features he had memorized from the image at his base. The woman was not too tall, but very broad, very strong, with a scar that ran from one cheek to the other, over the bridge of her nose. Her eyes squinted, both from the sun and from the smile she wore. Her tattoo covered her chest, a series of interlocking spirals centered on her right shoulder and stretching (bypassing her neck) to under her bottom left rib and down under her shorts. She helped Tuscus out of the boat.

Tuscus introduced himself and asked her name, knowing perfectly well it was Lemeca, but not wanting to suggest his contact's name in case he was mistaken. Tuscus' worry was unfounded. Her tattoo style was rare in this part of the world and no one would go through the trouble to reproduce it so exactly.

"I've been expecting you. You're a day late." She spoke with an affected Couoncil accent that she did not yet have down. "I kept a man watching for your barge on the shore down a bit. When he saw you, he woke me up. Good thing you had Jak as your captain. She's been coming to this camp for so long anyone could spot her a mile away. But she's not known for being late, and I'm not happy you are. What kept you?"

Lemeca had been at this facility for ten years. She had left the nursery not knowing what to do with herself, and after working as a clerk under various priests, she realized that she could not help trying to run the show everywhere she worked. Since she had no interest in the seminary, she knew she could only work behind the scenes for an incompetent priest. The problem was, there were far fewer priests to control than there were people who wanted to control them, most with better credentials than hers. Most of them had realized it earlier and had succeeded in annoying fewer of their bosses. So she had been fired time after time when her interests became obvious.

Fed up, she took the money she had saved (as a lay member of the Sailor's Church, she couldn't own property, just rent it, but she liked not being tied to a piece of real estate as she searched farther and farther afield for a job) and she had soon worked her way through it, since she hadn't saved too much. Soon her only option was showing up at the daily labor auction, starting as an hourly factory worker. The new plants the factories were running on did not require any real training beyond a half hour of instruction and she took to it quicker than most. Then, when she grew stronger, she became a dockworker, guiding and feeding the lifters, a job that paid a lot more, and was considered almost skilled labor. With the money she earned from that, she could move back into an apartment in a fairly young part of the town, and blow her money drinking.

When the plant capacity was expanded at the Semt mining camp, she applied for the post, in great part because rent for a cottage and food and beer were included in the pay. She didn't get a job at the plant, but they hired her to the mines, where she quickly made certain the foreman knew of her talent with numbers. The first one found her annoying and matronizing, so she was transferred to a man who appreciated her. Or rather, one who didn't mind delegating to her the more odious tasks. There she rose to be assistant foreman and remained so when he was promoted to a desk job which he couldn't do, supporting him as he was offered promotion after promotion. All the while she allowed him to submit her work as their own. They rose up through the ranks together, his incompetence masked by her own supreme skill.

Three years ago, she was approached by the Ducal Council's agents. They knew before she did of the discontent she developed languishing under useless (as she saw them) men and women. They assumed she would be of little use, just enough to check their books of the mine with hers, but then she came to organize the workers, spontaneously, and secreted stores slowly, items lost from the books, in shafts that showed up on old maps but had caved in on the newer ones. She felt appreciated as she had been by no one else when they came to her and asked her to head the entire operation, to recruit the workers to their side, to handle Council investments in the region.

Both the Ducal Council and the Sailor's Church had a lot of wealth invested in each other, some covertly, but most openly, as both held with the belief that rivalries should never get in the way of the most efficient (for the Council) or most profitable (for the Church) manner of doing business. She had been slowly building up a potential power base in the town, and she felt comfortable with her place in it. Lemeca had her entourage, a frill that she explained away as her handpicked agents. She had her headquarters deep in the mines, which she said she was preparing for her superiors when they would arrive someday. She had a treasury, skimmed at one percent added onto each transaction, (actually, the percentage varied between plus and minus ten percent, but the average worked out just in her favor). And she liked to pretend to herself that she was doing good, but when she couldn't, she convinced herself that she was bilking money out of people who were her enemies anyway.

She hated the messages from the home office, she hated them because she had to change what she was doing with every message, every message twisted her operation in ways she did not anticipate, and with every message she feared the inevitable reprimand. Or worse, a call to action, which she was not sure she could take, and which might be the end of her position as she became subordinate to whoever was placed in charge of the action.

XXXIII

Tuscus Makes a Deal

"Is there anyplace we can talk, anywhere away from here?" Tuscus said, "I need to tell you about that. I prefer to walk about when I talk."

"Come with me to the mine."

According to Tuscus' supervisors, Lemeca was an assistant foreman in the mine, nominal head of the night shift. The actual foreman preferred to delegate all his administrative duties and took upon himself both his and Lemeca's mining responsibilities. Tuscus must have broken into the middle of her sleep cycle, for she was walking unsteadily, brushing into the stalls selling cargo from the other boats. He waited until they had left the dock and were on the bridge to land. He hoped the way Jen looked after him was anxiety, maybe jealousy, though he had to make sure Jen could not hear him, just in case. Even though he doubted the priest would pay attention, he wanted at least the appearance of professionalism with Lemeca. A little envy couldn't hurt Jen, either.

"I was to bring you a message, yes?" Tuscus asked quietly, in a way Lemeca found amateurish.

"You were to bring me a message, yes. Where is my letter?"

"They wanted me to deliver the message in person, I don't have a letter for you. It's rather too important for something that could be lost. Now, what happened to me was this, we were 'ambushed'," he made sure that Lemeca heard the quotes, "By Council troops on our way here. And in this 'ambush', I came across a stash of weapons, left there for a very good reason, left there for me to find by our employers."

Lemeca sighed internally. This one was going to try to be clever, she thought. "Yes, yes, the message, what was it?"

"So, when we defeated the 'ambushers,' I commandeered the weapons. They are on Jak's boat now. You need weapons, don't you?"

"I don't need them now. I won't for some time."

"Trust me, you need the weapons. How much cash can you get by tomorrow? I'll reimburse you."

She didn't like the way this was heading. "What?" she asked, completely put off by this stream of instruction from a boy she had never met.

"Buy the weapons from me. What money I can't reimburse, I'll cover out of my expense account. But I have to make the transfer look legitimate."

"I don't need any weapons. I don't." The Council was after her treasury. That had to be what was happening. But what did they want with it?

"Trust me, you will, and soon."

"I trust you? Why? I just met you and you haven't even given my letter yet. You were carrying mail up here for that purpose, you know. Don't tell me they had you ship mail and you don't have a letter to give me. That's the way it's always been done, I get my letter with the rest of the mail. None of this word of mouth."

"My message is very simple, but if the letter was found, there would be trouble."

"You mean how?"

"I mean that what has to happen, might not. Especially if anyone knew too early."

He was being too clever, Lemeca thought. Didn't they teach him anything in those spy schools they had? "You still haven't told me what I need to know."

"You work the night shift, don't you?"

"Yes." she answered slowly, not sure where this was going, or why he was changing the subject. Still, if he was going to be coy and circumlocutious, she could do the same.

"How many people that you work with you think you can trust?"

"Oh, most of them."

"I mean really trust. I mean with your life, with this mine, with our bosses."

"Maybe half."

"Is that enough to run this complex with?" Tuscus waved his arm about, indicating the entirety of the iron processing operation.

"Sure. The bishop believes in heavy redundancy. I could

run the place with a quarter of a shift, no problem. The hydro plants are automated to a great extent, as is the scrubber and the mill. But why should I have to worry about that?"

"I told you. I met those troops of our employer's on our trip up here."

"Yes, yes, yes. I remember."

Tuscus finally realized that she was thoroughly exasperated. "In a bit, they will be coming up this way." He knew this wasn't true, but he hoped to be home and on his next assignment by the time Lemeca relayed that she was still expecting the troops. And then, hopefully, it will be seen as Lemeca's mistake and not his. "When they get here, the message for you is this: you are to revolt, petition the bishop for reasonable demands which she will reject, and then petition for entrance into the Ducal Council. Now, can you formulate a complaint which warrants armed insurrection?"

"What?" She couldn't believe what he had just said. She was to be usurped, and soon, it sounded like. It wasn't just her money that he was after, it was her power.

"Can you come up with any reason why you should revolt?"

"I understood that, what I mean is, what I mean is, what the hell are you talking about, revolting? I've heard nothing about this. I've heard no reason to begin thinking about this. We've been working so deep into this place for so long, why now?"

"Look, I don't make up the orders. I just transmit them." He hoped this was true, but the more he talked to Lemeca, the more he doubted his decision. "Is there a reason you could revolt?"

"I've quite a few, but…"

"Then, when the troops come, revolt. You won't have to do any fighting, don't worry. You just need to sit back and let the Oligarchy protect you. You know they can. We are close to the border, aren't we?"

"Not really. You have to go downstream, through Nephi, and then west a hundred miles or so."

"I mean straight across."

"You mean over land? Maybe ten miles. They can't get anyone here unless they airlift. You know how expensive that is? They'd have to bring in a huge fleet of dirigibles." Lemeca said.

"Do you know how much an iron mining and processing material is worth to them?" He didn't wait for her, instead, he answered for her. "Neither do I. But apparently it's worth the cost. You know the dirigibles could get here in less than a day."

Lemeca stood stock-still and thought. She didn't like her odds of getting out on this. "If they get this place, how will they get the iron out? Or food in?"

"I don't know. Like I said, I am just delivering the message."

"So who is supposed to run this thing?" It all sounded too confused to her. In her experience, the Council had never done things this haphazardly.

He thought quickly, trying his best to look as if he wasn't thinking at all. If he told her that he would be, she wouldn't believe him, as he was just a courier. If he said anyone outside, from home, she might take offense and might rebel against the Council for taking away her position. He took the safest route, the one she would definitely agree to, even if she didn't think it was rational. Unless she hated power, but then, if she did, she wouldn't be in the position she was in now.

"You are, of course," he said, "Who else would?"

"They are not bringing anyone else in?"

He shrugged. "Well, the troops."

"I mean besides them."

"No, no of course not. I mean, the troops will have their own commander, of course. You can't be expected to do that sort of stuff. You don't have the experience, do you?" He hoped he wasn't wrong, but his gut told him so. If she did, she might guess how much he was making up. But then she shook her head, and he almost sighed. "But the civilian aspects and the logistics, those will be your job. Don't worry about that. No one else has the experience here with the miners and other workers. I mean, do you think they would follow an Administrator immediately? It takes time to break through the brainwashing that the Church has put them through, and who better to do that then a Theocratic citizen, eh?" There, he hoped that sounded authentic enough, but it was a good response, he thought. Believable.

Lemeca shook her head imperceptibly, but she replied, "I suppose so. I suppose so." The message was probably being completely garbled by this boy, but it gave her an opportunity she had been waiting for all her life. If it failed, she supposed she could always blame him.

XXXIV

How Does This Man Get Around So Quickly?

Fennish had walked behind the Tuscus and Lemeca for some distance, not even bothering to hide, just lightening his skin a little (not too much, just enough) and giving himself a red welt to cover his cheek so he would not be immediately recognized. He heard Tuscus' proposal, and, though he hated to admit it, it was a clever recovery. Completely flawed, and he'd have to point that out the hard way, but at least he'd be able to put Lemeca's loyalty to the test while he ruined Tuscus. He knew who he would have to contact. Lemeca didn't know everything, or really anything, about the other Council agents in the town. The watchwords of the Oligarchy always had been redundancy, discretion, and efficiency and this post was no different.

Fennish, in his soul, knew that someone was watching

his every motion in any population center. He'd been sure he was alone on the raft, and he was right. He was wrong that anyone spied on him anymore. Occasionally someone would tail him for a bit, just clumsily enough to be noticed, but it was sufficient that he thought he was watched at all times. After all, the results were the same. He knew that whoever was watching would be pleased. When the Tuscus and Lemeca reached the mine and started to descend, he hurried after them, shifting color to match the walls, startling the switchman guiding a car out of the mouth of the mine.

XXXV

Jenaro Has a Job to Do Too, You Know

Jenaro had left the barge right after Tuscus to check in with the local parish priest. The temple was just as ugly as the other one in Nephi, but then, they had the same origin, and so what could he expect? He walked over the bridges toward it, and he was surprised to see armed men and women guarding each bridge. They nodded to him.

He was wearing the clothes he had brought with him, not the warmer (too warm) ones he had found. He had slept in those clothes, with their bizarre cloth, but they had given him nightmares, and so he had changed as soon as he found an outfit that was clean enough. The ones he had to choose from all were at least partial regalia. Even though the guards nodded, they still watched him as he walked away from them, he felt it. He watched them watch everyone, he saw them shift their gaze from one person to the other so quickly it seemed they were staring everywhere. He had not seen this before in the Theocracy. These were private police and whoever was paying for them must be horrendously scared or incredibly rich. Or both.

He reached the temple and entered. He found his way to the priest's office fairly quickly, and, for the second time in a week, he was face-to-face with one of the ubiquitous secretaries of the Church, the men and women rumored, probably correctly, to be the true rulers of the Church. This one was an elderly woman, so old she was showing it, easily near her mid-hundreds, possibly the oldest person Jen had seen in his life. The secretary greeted him, and he presented his credentials. She smiled at him.

"Sit, sit." she said. "The priest might be joining you."

Jen remained standing. "Might be?"

"He doesn't leave his office much. He doesn't see visitors either. Not recently."

"Could you please tell him that I'm here?"

"You don't worry about that, I already did. You might not be important enough for him to see you."

Jen rocked back a bit and looked at her with wide-open eyes.

"I don't mean you aren't important. Not in your own way. Just that his priorities are a little, well, different than a lot of people, even other members of the Church. It says here," she pointed to the credentials, "You know," she said, aggressively changing the subject, "You sound like a local boy?"

"Local enough, I suppose. I was born in Nephi."

"I came into Nephi with the Church. You must have been

there for that. You must have been very excited. I know it was for me. I just saw it from a desk after it was all over."

"Well, I was younger then, and I don't know. I certainly hadn't seen anything like it before or since."

She smiled. "I have, but it's thrilling every time. Converting the books from their systems to ours is something. Did you know they are very close? And the old records! Quite fun."

"I left for seminary soon after, so I didn't see much of it. I sometimes wish I did stay. To clean up after the chaos, you must feel like you conquered the world."

She nodded. "I did, I did, but then the feeling fades. The bishop was nice to me afterward. She sent me up here. She sent me here to put this camp in order too. I have been here ever since."

"Do you really like it here that much?" Jan asked.

She stared at him, but did not respond at first. The she said, with her fingers tensing, "You should go in, the priest will see you now."

"Excuse me?" he said, a bit taken aback by her change in manner.

"Go in." She turned to her desk, rather pointedly.

"Ok, fine."

He pushed the door open with a huff, and, as he turned to close it, he saw the secretary peer around the corner, then, as she saw him, she turned back to her work almost too quickly.

The room before him was a womb of red lacquer. There was no carpet, there was only his reflection in the floor, a reflection with few scratches, and he supposed it was either buffed religiously or it was fairly new, and he was right on both counts. The light came in through two windows, low to the ground, oval shaped, the glass a single pane taller than Jen in its smallest axis, both windows on either side of the desk. The desk was the same material as the floor, and seemed to merge into the floor. Unlike other offices he'd been in, there were no papers, no books, nothing at all on the desk save for a single letter opener with a steel blade and bone handle, carved into a tree, the roots balling to form the pommel, the branches and tendrils wrapping themselves to become the blade.

The man at the desk, obviously the priest, more obvious as he was in full ceremonial garb, almost a sin in itself, was staring at him. He was only a few years older than Jen, maybe in his early thirties at the outside, and he was a short man, with a large head, almost too large for his body. It seemed to be as large as his entire chest, held up only lightly by a whip-thin neck. His eyes were under bushy brows, and his hair was black and thick, rolling off his huge head, loosely curled. His cheeks were outlined by blue capillaries, a dark web against his almond skin. He stood up and walked around to greet Jen, and Jen presented his credentials again, and the priest didn't look at them, just smiled.

Jen stood still before the priest, and the priest then turned around and sat back behind his desk. He reached forward to pick up the letter opener, which he studied quite intently. Jen waited, hoping the priest would remember that etiquette required him to speak first. He stood still, the priest looked at the opener. He rocked back and forth on his heels, the priest rolled back and forth absentmindedly in his chair. When his feet were almost ready to give way, for Jen had tried his best to stand very still, and his calves weren't quite up to it, especially considering the walk of the day before, he coughed, and the priest looked up, smiled, walked around the desk to greet him, took a glance at his credentials, which he held still in his hand, sat down in his chair, and looked again at the opener.

"Um," Jen said, "Don't you want my report?"

"You have a report?"

"Well, I thought I was to report to you."

"You didn't?"

"Doesn't that mean telling you what happened?"

The priest smiled. ""You tell my secretary."

"But I've got important things to tell you, like we found a…"

"I don't want to hear it. Do you know how much I have to deal with?"

"Well, no," and Jen looked at his desk, imagining how it might look with something on it.

"Have you ever run an iron ore facility before?" He said "facility" with extraordinary emphasis, putting pride behind the word, as if he had just learned it.

"This is my first post."

"You just graduated seminary?" the priest said, accusingly.

"I took a little time off, but yes."

"Let me tell you, it is different here in the Real World. The teachers there have no idea what people like me have to handle on a day-to-day basis. What they don't know about labor management could fill this office! I tell you, they don't mention anything like how these people will take anything they can from you, they will take it and profit, at your expense. They want more and more. They try to sell to each other without putting it through me first. This operation doesn't get a cut of these private deals. They are just stealing money from me."

Jen's feet were hurting, but he was very confused. "I might not be understanding you, but isn't that what they are supposed to do? I mean, you should be proud of engaging in such holy work."

"For priests, you are right, for priests. For the people, you are wrong. They are to be guided by us. This is why we don't allow them to own any property."

"I thought that was to keep anyone who would affect the economy from being untrained, inexperienced, and creating excessive amounts of chaos." Jen felt like he was quoting his teachers. It made him feel uncomfortable. "It takes only a year to become a deacon. It's not like anyone can't do it with a little effort."

The priest shook his head. Jen was afraid that it would fall off. "No, no, no. You sound just like the bishop, and she does not want to acknowledge the reality of the situation. If these people had property, they don't just cause random fluctuations in the market, they tear it apart from the outside, like pirates raiding cities every minute of every day. And they are acquiring pirate capital here, or they were."

"You stopped this?" Jen wanted a seat. He couldn't believe what he was hearing.

"I stopped it. Of course I stopped it."

"How? I mean, we can't limit trade. You know that."

"I stopped it by fixing the currency."

"What? What do you mean, fixing the currency?" How,

Jen wondered, could this man so readily admit such blasphemy? Wearing full regalia to the office was bad enough, but this, this could cause him to be defrocked.

"What was happening was that they would reach the docks and buy the cargo from the boats before I could. Then they would sell it to each other and me, the cargo that was in addition to the items I had ordered. Well, I stopped paying them in cash and I made my own currency, which is quite beautiful, I must say, and I pay them in that. I know that they have some money secreted away, but they slowly spend it and soon they will have nothing but my scrip. Already they are buying from me, and me alone, everything they need to live. No one is getting any food through anyone else, and I own the inoculations, which I've started charging more for. I don't know why the bishop abides by the Matriarch's decision to sell them at cost. The inoculations are turning me a tidy profit. No one's ever brave enough to stop getting those."

"Um...That reminds me," Jen said, anxious to change the subject, "I and the crew of the ship I came in on needs theirs, just in case."

"Sure, but I don't deal with that. Go see the secretary, she'll fix you up."

"Um, I also have to ask you for accommodations."

"What? Didn't you arrange for those before you left. No matter, I have some fine hotels. "

"The problem is, see, I don't have any money."

"You don't have any money?" the priest said, shocked.

"A little, but not enough for a hotel."

"You question me on piety?"

"I was arguing theory."

"Get out of here."

"Where will I sleep?" Jen asked.

"Sleep where you can. In the river, for all I care. Ask the secretary. She might know a place for bums like you." He spat on the floor. "Look at that. Now I have to have the floor cleaned. Do you know how much that is going to cost me? Get out."

"So you don't want to know what happened on the river?"

"I could never begin to care."

Jen backed out of the office, looking at the priest who sat down at his desk, opened a drawer, pulled a cloth rag out (it was starched, with embroidery near the corners) and bent down to scrub the floor.

The secretary, when she saw him back out and shut the door quietly behind him, she smiled at him. "I want to know," she said.

"Know what?"

"I want to know what happened on the river."

"You were listening?"

She nodded. "I was. What happened?"

"Never mind. I don't think it's important anymore."

"Are you sure?"

"No. About the inoculations...and my room..."

"Send them here, we'll take care of it. You can sleep in the basement cells. I'm sure we have a closet big enough for you."

"Thank you."

He left the office, and saw the secretary bent down to her paperwork again.

XXXVI

Sometimes You Can't Go Back, Even If You've Only Been Gone a Little While

Jak had finished unloading the boat and she set her apprentices to watch the cargo. She took her husband's hand and walked off to wander around. She had been to the town many times, but each time was different. She knew, for example, that, after the first, no priest that had administered the place had ever lasted more than two years without going mad or committing suicide. The latest priest was one of the longest lasting, but even he had to give in at some point, and soon. Under the various priests, the policies that governed the place had changed from near anarchy to the current restrictions. She had never seen the police out in such force, especially not the plainclothes ones that prowled the crowds. Jen had not noticed them, he had been too shocked by the uniformed ones. And she knew that only the first priest, the only one to leave intact, had also been the only one to obey the bishop's will. All the rest saw her orders as too distant, too remote, too unaware of the problems to pay her any heed. But rather than speculate on this for too long, Jak was primarily concerned with finding alcohol, so she didn't think on it too much.

She crossed the bridge into the section of the town devoted to housing the miners. Her husband reminded her of a bar they had been to in the past, one they had wanted to return to, mostly for the food, but the drinks weren't too bad. They couldn't find it at first, but after asking a few people, and being watched closer and closer by the police, they managed to wind their way to it. The bartender was the same man that her husband remembered and remembered tipping extravagantly, something she had made fun of him for some nights after, and he blamed on a full stomach. She greeted the man and reintroduced her husband, though the man looked at her blankly. She ordered them drinks, and started to pay for them, but the bartender shook his head.

"I can't take those," he said

"I think I have something smaller." Jak's husband started rooting around in his pocket.

"It's not scrip. I have to take the scrip."

"It's good. You can test it for counterfeit if you want."

"I trust it. I could lose my bar if I take it. You see those people over there," he pointed to a male-female couple sitting a little too close to the bar, "Those people are police. If I sell you anything and you don't use the scrip, I get my lease killed."

"How are we to pay for this?" Jak asked.

"You can exchange your cash at the dock, but the rates

aren't that good. Only get what you think you need, because you can't change it back. The priest owns the moneychangers. He holds the monopoly tight. He's the one who prints the scrip. You try to exchange with anyone else, they lose their job."

Jak stared at him. "You can't be serious. You can't put up with this."

"We have no choice, we only get paid in scrip. No one will let you buy passage without the Matriarch's coin. No one will change to scrip to actual money. Anyone who does loses their license to dock here. We can't leave. We're trapped."

"He can't do that. I know he can't do that."

"It doesn't matter. He's the one with all the police. He's the one who transmits the bishop's will. Only him. The police can't argue, or they'll be excommunicated for not following the bishop. Worse, fired and blacklisted. He told them that the bishop told him so." The barman sighed. "We know that these rules don't come from the bishop..."

"Damn right they don't. I've dealt with her for years, and nothing like this ever had her stamp on it."

"The police have to do their job. They even like it, some of them."

The man and woman that he had indicated as police had been silent all that time, but then they rose and strolled over to the bar, holding their drinks in one hand, but with their static sticks dangling loose. They had been feeding them chunks of bread under the table so the little creatures could build up a charge quickly. They didn't take much feeding normally, but the spines on these were rippling slowly, in a languid, satisfied manner. The woman was short, very short, under Jak's armpit, but the man was average height. He stared at Jak and her husband in the back of their head at eye level.

"I don't care if the police are ordered to do that," she was saying, "I can't get a drink or do any sort of business here. You think I can get anyone to ship anything up here if they can't expect to bring home money that they can use?"

The bartender saw the police at that point and hung his head.

"You could always exchange it for some steel," the policeman said, "That's always a possibility."

Jen turned around and caught the policeman in the eye.

"Um, yes."

"And you really shouldn't imply that we don't do what is right, that we don't do our jobs. And you," he said, looking at the bartender, "You should stop pointing us out to everyone who comes in here. We've warned you before. You really want this place covered by someone new? We just have to tell the priest you're on to us, and we're gone. Now," he turned back to Jak, "Leave the bar please. You've already caused a stir and ruined these poor people's afternoon with unpleasant thoughts."

"She's sorry," Jak's husband said.

"I'm not," Jak said, "I mean what I said. You should be ashamed of yourself."

"Are you going to leave, ma'am?" the policewoman said, looking up at Jak's chin, her voice saying that Jak could say yes or no, but the response would be the same.

"She is, yes, yes she is," Jak's husband said, and he started to pull her to the door.

"No. I said no. I want to pay this man."

"Ok, as long as you're sure." The policewoman swung her static stick at Jak, the spines just grazing her skin through her clothes, and she felt the electricity poor into her system and she jerked and shook to the ground. Her husband kneeled down next to her, only to feel the stick on his cheek, lightly, not enough to draw blood, almost not touching, but then he was on the ground too, next to his wife, and they were clutching each other in the jolts that they couldn't feel, just shake to. The policeman looked at the policewoman hard, with a frown on his brow, and he pulled first Jak, then her husband out the door into the street outside the bar.

The policewoman stepped up to the bar and looked the bartender in the eyes. "Are you going to be quiet next time?" she asked.

XXXVII

Tuscus Thinks About What He's Done

Tuscus had emerged from the mine by this time, and he went back to his boat, feeling confident that his plan might save his life. Lemeca trusted him, or at least had appeared to. The brunch they had in the depths of her hideout confirmed that. And he wasn't too concerned about whether she deserved the potential double-cross, because the three full-time cooks she employed, and the porters, cleaning staff, and chef's assistants told him all he needed to know about whether she was being honorable with the money she was skimming from the Council. He knew the behavior was perfectly acceptable, if not encouraged in the Sailor's Church, but she had acquired the funds under the auspices of the Ducal Council and had to abide by their rules, even the ones of austerity. Of course, Tuscus wasn't following them, but then Tuscus was in disguise, and he thought that his extravagance was appropriate for the merchant personae he was putting on and he was telling himself that he wasn't enjoying one minute of it.

But he was by no means feeling guilty about the revolt they had been planning. After talking to her, he could half believe that she could pull it off using only the workers under her control. Apparently, there was enough internal dissent to cause the workers to rise up against the priest just as things stood. There was little need for agitation. She did not seem happy, actually, about the possible assistance of the Council troops. She thought that she would lose control in the process and she did not want that to happen especially after all the hard work she had put in. While she had needed to sleep for her upcoming shift (she complained that she was only getting half a night's sleep as it stood), he had left.

On his way to his cargo (he had to keep to his cover), he began formulating a plan to discuss with her. He would say that she should stage her revolt, and the troops would hide until they were needed. If, somehow, she could have her workers win on their own, she would retain leadership of them and the myrmidons would not show themselves. And then she would make demands, demands that were eminently reasonable but that the priest would deny. Since the priest was the voice of the bishop, and the bishop's eyes, he would only report what he wanted her to hear, in other words, that everything was fine, and crack down on the entire camp. The workers who weren't involved at first would surely join to fight against the police and the priest then. Then Lemeca could validly petition the Oligarchy for official help, as her grievances weren't being dealt within the Theocracy. It didn't hurt that the region was historically Council territory, nor did it hurt that the bishop was too far away to respond in person and ameliorate the camp conditions.

If she complained, he could always blame her for misunderstanding. She was, after all, a spy, but more than a spy, she was a traitor to her own government, while he, like all Oligarchy citizens, was a patriot by design, while she was attempting to undermine the regime of those who he had never served and she once had. Surely they would trust someone whose loyalties had never shifted over someone who was allied with them for expediency's sake. If she won, they would be happy. He could always say, again, that she was not following orders, that he delivered the message, if he had gotten his estimate of its contents wrong, something he was doubting less and less the more he thought of it.

Why else would the weapons have been where they were and the myrmidons there too if they weren't sleepers, or at least an oracle of the inevitable. If they were happy, his bosses would be pleased at his ingenuity. He should have known better, but being in Lemeca's presence while she discussed the potential for revolt had clouded his mind, as had his survival of the attack on the boat the previous day. He was beginning to believe himself invincible.

XXXVIII

It Must Have Been Something He Ate

Jen sat at the edge of the temple's platform, his feet dangling over, and he sang quietly to himself. On his right was his meal, half-picked over and half-forgotten. On his left was the report he was writing for the bishop. He knew she would want it rewritten upon his return, but he thought it a good idea to get the first and certainly rejected portion out of the way. It was difficult to concentrate on it, though. He felt as if he had seen, in that temple, images from his dreams, something that he could never describe, and certainly not to anyone who had never seen that basement gleaming in unnatural plasma light and metal. The language he had to write in, the formal legal tongue, chosen specifically for its impartial clarity, that language had never come easily to him, and it was worse still for him to discuss his impressions under that temple in it.

He could not begin to express killing a god, even a minor

one. The religion of the Sailor was not a monotheistic religion by any means. They acknowledged the legitimacy of the Ship, and of a few other, minor gods, but they still held all but the Ship in contempt. The Ship was reserved a special place in the pantheon, an object of veneration but not adoration, as it was widely acknowledged that the Ship was the progenitor god. The Sailor, from its vault under the cathedral in the holy city, had decreed that the other gods save the Ship deserved, not respect, but mere acknowledgment. The death of a minor god would possibly earn him a commendation, or it could earn him reprimand and banishment. Neither option appealed to him terribly much, neither option would give him any degree of anonymity. Still he knew he would write it up and let them do to him as they would when the time came.

Later that night, he dreamt. He saw the Sailor before him, almost as he imagined the deity. The god was striding across the land, each step creating a lake, rivers shooting out from each one to the next, beneath him a merchant fleet, the likes of which not seen since the god had been alive, floating along these flying rivers. The god's eyes looked up into the sky, out to what he said was the god Ship, the god the Sailor worshipped, but the god it had overthrown, the god it had replaced in all respects, surpassing what the old deity had been a thousand-fold, as the Sailor was born human, born from the wombs that dwelt in the hidden caches, those large, fleshy masses that sat pulsing until the child is disgorged down the sluice. He saw the Sailor in its first revolt against the duchies that had tried to take the Sailor's profits, who had abused the Sailor's workers. He saw the Sailor, still walking the land and ocean like the god the Sailor was, he saw the Sailor take the people and turn them against their masters, to teach them life independent of the rule of the duchies. He saw the Sailor rise up into the skies, to enter into the Ship he had worshipped and come down no longer human, but a god.

Like all gods, the Sailor was immobile then, but who needed to move when a god was everywhere in their domain. The advantage of any god was the omniscience and omnipresence and omnipotence under their auspices, and the Sailor's mercantile empire expand further under its first Patriarch, the man who had loved the Sailor, the man who some say went mad when the Sailor deified himself, and who could no longer physically express his love, taking out his anger on the rest of the world, the anger of a man who can not be with the one he loves, though the object of that love is right before him. He saw the history then of the Sailor's Church, all as he had learned in Seminary, the land expanding and contracting, reduced to its core islands, increased to its current state, almost at the peak, all the while the Sailor watching, huge and embracing the sea, the rivers, the rain, the clouds, the sky and stars, standing tall on the island capital of the Theocracy, the holy city where the Sailor's Church had stretched across the waters.

This was the dream that Jen had most often, though like any dream, he did not remember it when he woke, he only could recall parts, vague aspects that were lost as the day progressed. But here, the dream changed, here, the god receded, and the world rolled beneath Jen until he saw a crater lake and a processing facility at its base. He saw a lake with blood roiling through it, he saw a fire spreading, consuming the metal rolls, he saw a fist come from the west, and a fist from the east, both rising above the town, both holding water in the cup of their hands, but both getting in the way of the other, while beneath, the land burned, until the crater itself cracked open and water flooded the land beneath it, the force of the water washing away everything he could see, the trees themselves stripped nude of bark and leaves, their naked tendrils whipping about each other, desperate to consume each other for what little nourishment they could extract.

In the middle of the crater, one that was deep and the water flowed for a very long time, seemingly nonstop, but of course it stopped, though the boiling in the air was strong, he thought he saw a gleaming metal city, and as he swooped down to it, he could see it clearer and clearer, but then he woke up.

XXXIX

Some Days, It Just Doesn't Pay to Get Out of Bed

When he woke up, he heard cries from outside, loud cries, resonating through the walls, into the water-surrounded cell he was sleeping in. He pulled the door open, and the hall was empty. He could only see the ripple of the water through the windows, he could only watch it glow from the sun, so he knew that the day had begun, but he did not know the time, whether he had woke too early or whether the building was unusually deserted. He found his way to the first floor, and made his way through the deserted rooms. By that point, he knew something was wrong, as he knew that there should be someone in the offices, someone to stay watching the building at all times and deal with emergencies as they could arose, but he was not scared. Instead, he was curious. The shouting was louder, a chant almost, ragged but with a beat, repeating over and over again, breaking its iterations only briefly.

Then he got to the front of the temple, not seeing anyone at all, and he walked through the front door, and there, above him, was the man who had talked to the day before, the parish priest, the one who had dismissed him and insulted him and hurled him from his office. There was the man, but the man didn't know it, and Jen was sick staring at him, he turned away.

His eyes went back to him of their own accord, and his gaze slid up a newly-erected pole, so bloody and damp still, though turning brown as the blood dried, up the pole to where the crust of blood was thicker and thicker still, to the truncated neck and head of the parish priest, his face torn into an expression of anger and hatred, his eyes ripped out, crying tears of blood, but still fierce and scared in their absence, his mouth in a grimace that showed his bright white teeth, the only part of his face not covered in blood. Jen turned his gaze away and looked to the shore, where he heard the chants become cheers of triumph.

Under the door, near the pole, he saw the secretary, and she was crying. He went to her, and he saw that her tears were running over a wide smile.

"He's dead, he's dead. That bastard is dead. Can you understand how much we all hated him? Can you understand how much we all wanted to kill him? I have never thought of hurting anyone before. I lusted after his death. I knew he deserved it."

"How could you want him dead?" Jen asked. "He was a priest, he was a human."

"You do not understand. You just dealt with him for a half an hour on one day. You do not know the pain he's put everyone here through. You do not know the amount of maiming he caused in his stay, more than anyone else. He tore these people apart. He gave them nothing in return but more pain."

"I'll give you that he was incompetent..."

"Incompetent!"

"Ok, maybe more, but he was still a person. There must have been other ways to solve this than with killing the man."

"No," she said with finality.

"How can you be sure?"

"I am sure. I am sure of this. We could have done something else, but we didn't want to. He could have lived, but people don't kill other people for because it is efficient, but because they lust for it. I lusted for his death like nothing else since he arrived. You know what it is like to want nothing more than to have someone die, to take joy only in thoughts of death, to not be able to think beyond this obsession? You imagine a town like this. You imagine living here like this. You tell me if we were justified, you sanctimonious shit."

"We? We? You were one of the ones who killed him?"

"No, I didn't kill him. I wasn't even awake. But I support those people who did. I might as well have been involved. I wish I had been. If I could have seen his face as he died, that would have been worth everything to me."

"But you worked with him, you knew him. How could you kill someone who you saw every day, who you knew as well as you did him?"

She wiped her tears and looked straight at Jen. "It was

because I knew him that I feel this way. If I didn't have to deal with him, I would never have wanted to kill him. I would not be sitting here, just looking at that head. I'm going to leave that thing up until it rots off the pole. I'm going to find the skull, wherever it lands. I'm going to make it into a paperweight for the next priest. I told you they've been getting worse as the years go on? The skull will remind them to be civil, or at least more than that was," she looked up at the head, and spit up at it, the spit landing in the water, falling short and wide of the pole.

"How do you know there will be another priest here, how do you know the people who did this, who killed one priest, will want a replacement?"

"What's the alternative? A priest has to be here."

"If you are in the Theocracy, yes. But do these people, the people mistreated enough by him," he pointed at the head and paused, "Do these people want to remain in a system that treated them so poorly?"

"You tell me, young father. Who would be the priest, hypothetically?"

"I'm not sure. You would know better than I would. Was he the sole owner of this mine?" Jen looked back up at the head.

"The majority of the shares are owned by local deacons. I own maybe one percent, the bishop owns about thirty percent, and he owned maybe ten."

"Those shares are open to anyone then, right?"

"They might revert to the bishop. I think that was in the contract that put the bishop here. She could keep them and work from here, and give up her shares in Nephi, or she could appoint a parish priest and stay down river."

"Then whoever bought those stock would be the parish priest."

"We need someone in the interim," she said.

"Is there anyone here who would do?"

"Yes. I could do it. But I'm not a priest, just a deacon. Like everyone else in the Church around here. You are a priest, aren't you Father?"

"Brother. I'm just out of seminary."

"It doesn't matter. Now, I have an idea."

Jen knew what it was, and he didn't like it one bit. "No."

"It will only be for a while."

"No."

"Until the bishop appoints a replacement."

"The people won't like the idea of having another priest to replace the one they just killed?" Jen asked.

"We just went over that."

"I've only been here a day."

"You are the only priest around."

"I don't know anything about running this place, especially not while it's under rebellion."

She patted his arm. "You won't have to. I can do most of it."

"So then what do you need me for? You have a share of this place. More than I do. You are a more legitimate choice."

"I told you. I'm not a priest. The bishop will want a priest in charge. Look at it this way. I'll recommend to the bishop that you get a piece of this place. She'll listen to me. I know she will. She has in the past. She'll owe you for keeping the Church's presence in the region."

Jen did not like the idea. It would give him more money than he would know how to give away. If he lived. If the people did not want to kill him too. He already was apprehensive about leaving the temple wearing his raiments.

"No. I wouldn't deserve it."

"In less than an hour, the rest of the people who work in this building will be here. What should I tell them?"

"I don't know."

"I could tell them to go home."

"Sure. That's a good idea."

She sighed. "They'll go and sit at home and start thinking. They'll be panicking. They won't be able to do anything. They will be sitting at home scared."

Jen shrugged. "Then don't tell them to go home."

"Are you suggesting that they stay here?"

"I don't know."

"We can put them to work."

"You can put them to work."

She said thoughtfully. "That will keep their minds off of what happened."

"Maybe. If you think so."

"What should I have them do?"

"I don't know. Whatever you want them to."

"I will. Thank you, Father."

"Brother. Hey, what..."

"You've been most helpful."

"No, I haven't."

"You should really get into your office."

"I don't have an office," Jen insisted.

"The old priest was always late to work. No one liked that. You should be early."

"I don't know what..."

"You don't want happened to him to happen to you, would you?"

"You are really..."

"Go in now."

"Yes, ma'am."

Jen turned and went into the temple, looking as he pushed the door open, his back against it, looking at the head on the post, and he shut the door behind him, his eyes closing with the door.

Jak slept in that morning, she didn't need to rise, the merchant had bought passage both ways, and he was planning on staying in the mining town for some time longer. She was in the cabin of the barge, the passenger cubicles that had been put in place for Jenaro and Tuscus taken down to expand her and her husband's sleeping space, and they were enjoying the extra room. The former floorboards were against the walls to block any noise from outside.

It was late morning, almost noon, when they finally awoke, feeling much better, much more rested. They stood up and they had room, a feeling they relished, for they could so rarely stand in their cabin. They talked of the years when they no longer needed to work, and how they would always leave the space so large. Of course, they knew that they would never retire. They already had more than enough money to do so, but they did not want to wake up everyday with nothing to do. Just on occasion.

Her husband opened the door and walked out on deck. He called Jak immediately. She joined him and exclaimed loudly. They locked up the boat and went to find their apprentices and their passengers.

"We are not staying around to be killed," she said to her husband, "We are leaving now. The profits be damned. Tell them I'll even give them passage for free."

Tuscus also slept in late. He was deep in the mine, in the headquarters Lemeca had shown him the day before. He had slept fitfully, the noise outside his room disturbing him, but not enough to wake him. When he did open his eyes, it was to silence, which was too unusual for him to remain asleep to.

The room was black, far too black. He could barely see the flicker of a glow where the lights had been, the residual heat the only thing he could perceive. He found his way to the door by following the wall and he turned on the lights, blinding himself. He was still looking at the dead filaments when they came to life.

He dressed slowly after bathing, he had no need to hurry, and he was thankful for running water after the barge, where the river simply did not compare. He didn't try to think of how the water got this deep in the ground (it was collected from pipes that ran the pneumatic drills in those periods at shift changes when the drills weren't working, while the electricity used for the lights and heating the water was tapped off of the power lines that lit up the mine), he just enjoyed it very much.

When he did leave, he opened the door to a brightly lit

hallway, all the lights on full. It was unlike the day before, when the halls had been dim, according to Lemeca to keep the power drain from being noticeable. He searched for Lemeca, but he could not find her, or anyone in the headquarters, or rather, no one who looked familiar or looked as if they might know where Lemeca might be. He went to the elevator, he rode it to the surface, taking with him nothing, for he expected to be back down later in the day, at least to sleep.

He left the mine, and the first sight he had was Lemeca, who he greeted casually.

"Thank you so much," she said.

"For what?"

"I have to say, I doubted you. I thought you were wrong. I know now that you were telling the truth."

"Always. Always. About what?"

"Don't be like that."

"Like what?"

"Don't be so modest. You promised them, here they are."

Tuscus looked beyond Lemeca (they had walked out of the mine by this point) and he saw tall and short bald, sexless creatures, all with three eyes, all carrying Oligarchy weapons, and Tuscus, he felt sick, but he smiled.

"Of course. What did you expect?"

"They showed up last night, after you went to sleep."

"They were a bit early, but you have to love the efficiency."

"When they arrived, we took the village."

His mind screamed, but he smiled. "Oh, did you?"

"Yes. The place is now ours. The priest is dead."

His stomach really twisted itself. "Which priest?"

"The parish priest, of course. Is there another?"

"Yes, yes there is." He thought quickly. He had no choice. "There's a young one, my age and he's to be left alone. There are plans for him." That should be sufficiently vague.

"I'll pass the word."

"Thank you."

"No, thank you. So much. You don't know what you've done here."

"I'm sure I don't."

At this point, Jak's husband came through the crowd and reached Tuscus.

"Come with me."

"And who are you?" Tuscus said.

"Jak's husband. Don't you remember? I was on the barge with you on the way here."

"Don't you have a name? Introduce yourself to the lady." He gestured to Lemeca.

"Come on."

"I'm not going anywhere."

"He's not going anywhere," Lemeca said. She had been listening, but she felt the need to reinforce Tuscus' decision.

"We're leaving, we're leaving. Jak doesn't want to die, and neither do I."

"No one's going to die," Lemeca said.

"You don't know that, you don't."

"Yes, I do." Lemeca said.

"She'll make sure of it, won't you? No one will die. No one has to. We are all perfectly safe," Tuscus said.

"I don't care. I've read of things like these, and they can't end up well."

"You're being paranoid," Lemeca said.

"Yes, he is, isn't he," Tuscus said.

"This is your last chance. Do you honestly think the bishop will just let this go? Do you think she can afford to? What will you do when her troops come up that river and start taking this place back, what will you do?"

"He stays. We need him here," Lemeca said.

"You heard her. I am staying. I think they are right, and I think that your naysaying can only hurt what these people are trying to do," Tuscus said.

"Suit yourself," and Jak's husband walked back through the crowd to the temple where he knew Jen was staying.

The doors of the temple were open, just as they had been the day before. The clerks were bustling to and fro, ignoring him, ignoring what might be happening outside, even the head that was on the post, a head which had given him pause, though he did not know whose it was, he still did not like the look of the thing. He knew it could not bode well. He thought to himself that maybe they left it up as a totem to ward off further assaults, perhaps they had sacrificed the man, whoever it was, as a preemptive method of preventing their own deaths, though he thought the head looked as if it had been up during the night, at least the blood was dry.

The clerks were very glad that the parish priest had died. The most pacific one of them had dreamed the same thing, deep in their hearts, and the enactment of their desires caused not a small amount of trauma as they reconciled the joy they felt with the eyeless head they saw on the pole. Jak's husband worked his way through the halls of the temple, asking everyone he could if they knew what had happened to Jen. Most looked at him blankly, but one clerk with bright eyes and a contemplative expression on her face directed him to the parish priest's office, though he did not know how Jen could have ended up there.

He arrived at the office, at the front of the place, and he encountered the secretary there. She smiled at him, until he asked where Jen was.

"Why do you need to know?" she asked.

"Jen needs to come with me."

"He's needed here."

He tried to be firm. "We are leaving, and he is coming with us."

"No, no, he's not. He will stay."

"Could I see him?"

The secretary smiled. "No."

"He can decide for himself."

She looked at him, right in his eyes and out the back of his head, with the force of a century of civil servitude. She paused, then said, "I can decide for him."

"Please."

"Ask all you want, I won't change my mind."

"Shouldn't he know that we are leaving?"

"I'll tell him."

"I'm sure he will want to hear it from me."

"I'm sure it won't matter. He's staying here. Do you understand?" And she rose a little in her seat behind the desk, not much, just a few centimeters, just enough for him to see a little more of her and her unhappy expression, for him to see the strain that was not in her face but was instead in her hands and lower arms as they shook a little back and forth.

"Yes. Yes, I do."

"Good," she rested back down in her chair, but her arms still shook, "Leave now, please."

And he did, and he made his way back to the boat without Jen or Tuscus and did not look forward to breaking that news to Jak.

Back to the Scene of the Crime

Jak was walking through the residential part of the camp, where they had been the day before for their drink. Her apprentices had met some people who lived in that part of the camp not five trips ago, and they still had not worn out their own novelty or welcome. The couple they stayed with seemed to like drinking with them, and the apprentices reported that they needed to only entertain them with stories of their adventures on the river and in Nephi for free food and housing. It was quiet, just as quiet as the day before, but the quiet was one that she did not want to feel behind her.

She felt it haunting her at every intersection, on every street. The residential area was a poorer version of every housing setup she had ever seen, with houses and small stores, selling only food and household goods, every few feet. The stores and bars were set out from the rest of the houses with blue paint on their front face and red on their rear. Paths wound between them, worn into existence from use alone, with the houses separate from the streets where lifters walked, their huge clumsy bodies carrying the goods that the markets needed on their shoulders or in wheelbarrows. The lifters were all she saw out on the streets, except the police.

The houses ranged from a hole leading into the ground to structures five or six stories tall. There were a few house trees already inhabited, though they had only come on the market half a century before. But then, the Ducal Council, which had owned this region at that point, was more likely to implement such things. In fact, it looked like quite a few had been planted in groves near the edge of the camp, and they were growing robustly, though not yet old enough to be occupied. She went from house to house, asking for the people her apprentices were staying at, but very few would open their doors, and far fewer would answer her questions as she asked directions.

She did find them, finally, by knocking on the door of the women they were staying with. The woman who answered the door looked scared, the apprentices looked excited. They left with her almost immediately, for they had been waiting for her to arrive, expecting her sooner than she showed up, but were not being too impatient about it.

As she left and mounted the bridge for the part of the center of the town on the lake, she saw two police officers, the same ones that had accosted her and her husband the day before. They nodded and smiled at her when they saw her looking at them. They waved her over to them.

"You going to be back?" the policewoman asked.

"No. I don't think so."

"What is your business over there?"

"I'm leaving town. I'm going down river."

"You sure you want to do that?" the policewoman asked.

"You aren't quite showing solidarity with the workers," the policeman said.

"This is supposed to bother me?" Jak asked.

"It would be nice if you would support them," the policewoman said.

"I don't even know what you're talking about. In fact, I don't care either way."

"You should." the policeman said.

"Are you going to tell me you don't care about the way these people are trying to get justice?" the policewoman said.

Jak said angrily, "You didn't yesterday. You could care less about justice yesterday. You were taking this justice away from them yesterday."

The policewoman sighed and recited, as if she was going to repeat something she had said many, many times.

"We have a job. We keep the peace. That is our job. How and why and where, that is for someone else to decide. But the job must be done, by us or someone else. We would rather be the one who does it than be the one it is done to, like you. We are apolitical. We could care less for what the rules are, as long as I can enforce them. As long as the rules are clear. As long as the rules are rules, and uniform. This is what we do and we do it well, thank you."

"I'm going to my boat and leaving. And these two are coming with me," Jak responded.

"I can't let you," the policeman said.

And she walked onto the bridge, and they stood there and watched her go.

"Stop," they yelled, but they did not move.

"Go no further," they yelled, louder, but still, no movement.

"You may not leave," but she was off the bridge, still walking with her steady, calm gait, her black skin reflected in the water, her apprentices behind her like trailing wings.

"Halt," they yelled, loudest of all, but nothing responded, not even those in the buildings around them who surely heard them, only her, and she strolled around the corner of one building and mounting the bridge to the next, her boat fairly close.

When they were aboard the boat and were waiting for her husband, Jak grilled her apprentices.

"Did your friends know what had happened?" She addressed the question to the elder, in the traditional manner of speaking only to the senior apprentice. Jak actually found it a bother, but the two of them insisted, and she could not argue with them on it. The younger just ignored her, and the older got quietly mad. She supposed she could push the issue, but it would have been greater trouble than it was worth.

"They didn't, not really. They said that one of the assistant foreman, what was her name?"

"Lemeca." the younger said.

"Lemeca, right, Lemeca killed the parish priest. She's taken over the mining, the smelting, the whole bit. She's having everyone go to work. The police are keeping the streets clear."

"I can understand why everyone is scared."

"I can't. They say this Lemeca is an asshole. They also say she is at least honorable. More than the priest."

"But she killed the priest. She could kill again."

"We've seen you kill too, remember. We're not scared of you," the younger interjected.

"But that's different. You work for me."

"From what I heard, the priest deserved it," the eldest said.

"No one deserves it."

"Death happens to everyone. And like she said, we saw you kill those things on the river."

"In my own defense."

"You know that Lemeca didn't? I mean, they say she was a controlling little ass (one of our friends had had a shift under her, you know, and she transferred as soon as she could, but still), but they think she'll do a better job than the priest. Even if life is still a little shitty. But not as shitty as under the priest, which is all they care about now."

Jak responded, "Give them a couple weeks under Lemeca and they'll want to go back to the old way."

"They are happy now," the elder apprentice said.

XXXXI

He's Oblivious, Isn't He?

At the end of the day, the secretary opened up the door to Jen's new office. He had spent the day reading, mostly the history of the region, all of which he had read before, but it entertained him. Occasionally, the secretary came in with papers for him to sign, and he did so after reading them in what he hoped seemed to be a close manner. He understood none of them, but he felt that no one else did either, so he wasn't put out by that. He spent the rest of the day staring out the windows, standing still in front of them, a human pupil in them, and watched the activity on the shore, activity he did not understand, but that did not bother him.

The secretary told him that it was time for him to leave.

"You should stay here," she continued, "It might not be safe for you to leave."

"Maybe you are right. My stuff is still here?"

"We kept it in the same cubicle. We could move you to a larger room if you like."

"No, thank you. That would be wasteful. I don't think you should go home either. Maybe you should take the larger room."

"Thank you, I will." She sounded grateful, but it seemed she had been expecting him to offer it to her.

"Oh, did anyone come for me? Any messages?" he asked, jokingly.

"Not really. One man did."

"Who? Was it important?"

"Of course not. I would have brought him into you if it was. Did I do wrong?"

"No. No. Look, I know I haven't done much today, but I'm tired. Just point me to some food and then bed."

"Of course."

XXXXII

Jak Does the Responsible Thing

Jak was not panicking. She rarely did. She knew what she had to do, though she would rather have run all the way to Nephi. She knew she had to try to contact the bishop's outpost along the river at the closest point to the border, which is what she should have done when they were ambushed on their way up, but then, she had not wanted to damage her reputation for being able to deal with anything and protect her clients at all costs. Her husband and apprentices had known of her responsibility, but they knew better than to suggest it to her. The priest and merchant obviously hadn't thought of it, though the priest should have known and the merchant would not have bothered, and that did not bother her. This time, though, with a revolt in progress, there was no shame in it, and she had done most of her job. This time, also, there was certain to be a reward that would compensate for the forms she would have to sign and the testimonies she would have to give. The bishop was usually very good about such things.

Jak's crew was working overtime. They had left Semt as quickly as possible, and by mid day had made it to the outpost. The outpost itself was a small building in the middle of a cove that had been artificially deepened to match the depth of the river. About half of the outpost was underwater, and she could see the pylons descending below it. It was just the size of a small temple, and it had a makeshift porch added onto its back, as well as a plank bridge to the shore, both sloppy continuations of the dock in its front.

Three barges, similar to hers, were tied to it. They drifted idly and stank of grain alcohol. The air in the cove was fairly still, much more so than the river as a whole. A tower rose out of its roof, made of dried, cured, and straightened roots. It was taller than the forest around the cove by half again and remarkably free of any growth, a task that must take up most of the outpost's staff's time, Jak thought, especially as it was the perfect height for the strangle branches of the nearby trees. It was almost, but not quite, out of their reach. The tower was mere scaffolding, with a large dumbwaiter dangling down its center. Attached to it at the top was a dirigible, all three of its bags fully inflated and gleaming black, straining at the rope that tied it to the tower, a rope that would be tautest directly before sunset and loosest before sunrise, but, in any case, a rope which held the gondola's entrance level to the dumbwaiter's floor. The twin rotors on its engine rotated idly with the breeze.

The outpost seemed quiet, as they pulled up, and they heard only low talk. When they came closer and tied up, a man leaned over the roof's edge and called down to them. Jak explained as best she could, and the man replied that the captain would be right down. Another man jumped off the roof to land in the water and he swam up to the barge, climbed on to it, and led Jak inside.

Inside, the place was cluttered, very cluttered, with stacks of paper in the corners and a radio hanging from the ceiling. Jak tried not to stare at it, but she hadn't seen too many. She soon realized that it was broken, for even her inexpert eye could tell that plants growing out of it weren't good for the electronics within. The captain led her into his office, which was more a corner with blinds around it and a nice view of the cove, and there, he was kind in his listening. He said "mm-hmm" at all the appropriate points. He asked her very pointed questions, very quickly, and she answered as best she could, though she didn't feel rushed. When he was done, he sat her down with a bank of paperwork, and, as she filled it out, she heard him vaguely, indistinctly, question her crew and her husband. Then the voices changed, and she heard grunting and clunking. The captain stepped in on her again and smiled.

"Thank you very much for telling us this. It would have been a few more days before we found out otherwise. We have to send the dirigible down to Nephi to carry word to the bishop. She will want to know."

"Well, good. I'm glad I was able to be some help."

"We have a favor still to ask from you. If you don't mind."

"No, not all," Actually, Jak did mind, but she knew who she needed to appease, and she knew that if she didn't, she might be harassed in port a little more often. If there was still a Semt to make runs to afterwards and he didn't force her to change her route altogether. She could guess the favor, and she knew she would say yes before he asked, in a sheepish voice, which she knew was a front, for he would make her say "Yes," even if she told him "No."

"Could we borrow you and your barge?" the captain asked.

XXXXIII

Mornings Are Just Miserable All Around

For the second morning in a row, Jen woke up to the sound of yelling. These were more panicky than the first, but Jen took his time getting ready. His bath was long and cool, he just lounged below the water, reading, as the shouts got louder and then died down.

He had ended up sleeping in the parish priest's office. It was the largest non-public room with its own bathroom, and though he had protested when the secretary suggested it, he had given in when she insisted over and over again that it was the best place, as it would seem he had been working all night and would inspire the clerks. She had supplied him with books from the temple library (he had chosen a light adventure novel, not really important, but important books rarely tend to be enjoyable. Or even instructive. Or, for that matter, important) and the cot from the cell he had stayed in before.

As he was dressing and snacking, the shouting erupted again. He walked to the large eye window in the office and stood in the center, looking out, the pupil in a cat's eye, and he saw the movement of the people on the shore, anxious and nervous in their movements. He hurried up getting dressed and then went outside to run toward the mine's shore.

He saw three boats on the river and, above them, a dirigible. He stopped on the bridge that led from the temple, letting the little traffic there was flow past him. He grabbed at the railing loosely, letting it just rest against his fingers. The dirigible pulled over the land, hovered over the ore processing plant, its propeller only going fast enough to keep it from drifting from its position, where everyone was looking up atit. On each of the boats, the three barges, he saw five of the carapaced troops he knew to be the Church's more elite guard. He thought that they must be the bishop's personal guard, almost all of it. There, in the water, he saw, from a familiar boat (was that Jak's boat? He was shocked to see it again, but it was hers. He could tell from the scarring on the cabin where the wood had blackened from the flaming arrows), four carapaced creatures, wearing armor similar to the one that he and Tuscus had found in the temple, gather about a fifth, and they chanted louder and louder until the very air around him was rippling.

Then, with a shout, reality itself rippled away from him, and he was separated by nothing from it. He tried to move, but he was in a shell the shape of his body that he could not break. He could move his eyes in his head, and he felt no need to breathe, but his attempt to turn his head was met with impossibility. The entire shore was full of frozen people, people half in step, people loading ore into hoppers, people drawing the weapons that looked so familiar. He saw the shellbacks leap from the boat, still in a circle, and drift through the air, almost too slow to stay up, toward the shore twenty yards away.

As they jumped, he saw the taller three-eyed creatures drop back, with the smaller ones scurry forward, raising their crossbows to aim at the fifteen shapes arcing through the air towards them. Then the bolts let fly, all hitting one carapace, slowing it, knocking it back, and then another target and a third, and then the archers slipped back to join their taller brethren, and they walked almost casually to the mountains. With three splashes, the hit templars splashed in the water and twelve others landed on the shore, moving as fast as demons but still slower than the strolling myrmidons. The carapaces swept toward the retreating creatures.

People were beginning to move again, some falling to the ground, some drawing weapons. In the midst of the greatest clusters of these, from the air ship were thrown small tumbling spheres that burst above their heads and fell in fire on their now-running bodies.

Another group of people tried to block the myrmidons, but the myrmidons ignored them. One stuck at the leg of one of the three-eyed creatures with his sword, perhaps out of frustration. The myrmidon did not stop, did not pause, but instead tossed the man into the air, cut off his leg at the knee, caught the calf on its way down, and started chewing on it, limping a little at first but less and less as the gash in its leg healed. The man fell to the ground where he lay bleeding, his remaining leg twisted behind him.

The dirigible started to move towards the myrmidons, overtaking the carapaced ones, flinging the bombs ahead, missing them. And then the myrmidons were gone, disappeared as if they had never been there, leaving the shellbacks and the rebels on the ground alone.

From the carapaces' arms and heads, fire flowed like a river down and along the ground, puddles of it burning in their footsteps. Most of the rebels had laid down their swords, and those were ignored by the shellbacks, but a few had gathered around Lemeca, guarding her as best they could.

XXXXIV

Lust for Life

Then, across the way from Jen, near the rebel miners, Tuscus opened his eyes, because he could move again, and, though he wanted to shut them, he could not keep them so. He heard the sound of the workers dying in the fires, he heard them as they were covered with the flaming liquid and lost themselves to the blaze. He felt the heat on his face, he smelled the blood as the workers attacked the carapaced ones and had their limbs cut clean off. He could not avert his gaze, he could not keep his eyes shut any longer. He opened his eyes and, from his place against the mouth of the mine, he saw.

He had seen death many times in the past, he had killed many times himself. But those were members of the Oligarchy, and they were designed to be killed, practice dummies, so to speak. Sure they were alive, sure they though and felt, but no more than a fish. They were base animals and by no means sapient. They were programmed not to be, after all. But these folk, those people dying, the workers, they were sapient. He knew that. He knew they were. It was part of his training, after all, that the Church sent sapients to do robot work, a cruelty that was never perpetrated in the Oligarchy and never would be.

Because they were sapient, they were able to revolt, something that had not happened for two millennia in the Ducal Council. Civil disorder was unheard of, police were unnecessary. Any discontents were purged long before they left the nursery, and the years had culled almost them from geneset altogether. But these people, he had coerced them into revolt. Their sapience let them die, not as machines with their use fulfilled, killed at the end of their utility (though if properly programmed (as more and more were) they expired naturally after a few weeks of idleness), out of kindness, euthanized and cloned if they were successful designs, debugged if they weren't. These sapients, the workers before him, they died a useless death. A death that he was watching, noticing immediately that those who dropped their weapons were not hunted and those who attacked were killed. He knew the Council would not be so malicious as to let these people live with such a failure, he knew they would have killed the revolutionaries before they had to live their lives in the shame of their defeat, and he hated the Theocracy for what they were doing to their own people.

He wanted to cry, he wanted to bawl his eyes out. At the very least, it would blur his vision, smoothing the images before him into a great ripple of light, but he could not get the tears to come to him. He knew that he was the cause, he knew these people were dying because of him, because of his mistake, his simple mistake of losing a letter and then making up a story to cover it up. He supposed he could rationalize it by pretending to himself that they would die anyway, and those who did were rebels, untrustworthy and dishonorable by nature, and they would die in the same way in some future revolt if they weren't dying as he watched.

But he knew he was losing them to his incompetence, to his failure and his unwillingness to die for his failure. His own life lust, for that is how he saw it now, killed them. It was not something as pure as love, no, it would not give itself, it was simple lust, designed only to take from others to feed itself. His own life lust was behind his pretensions to duty. He had destroyed all chance that the Oligarchy had had to recover this mine, rightfully theirs for so many years, even if it was only recently exploited, and he had destroyed a decade and a half of work that had gone into this place, the slow infiltration that was obviously not ready yet. But then, fifteen years was nothing to the Council, nor to the Church, it wasn't even the age of maturity, a child would still be in a nursery after such a short time, how could the plans that two nations worked take only fifteen years to complete?

But he could not cry, just as he could not close his eyes. The image in front of him, playing out slow, to his mind, was one that froze him, which shook him into silence and immobility. In reaction, he could not stop it, that was the last thing from his mind, the only resistance to it was his subconscious, his skin shifted color to match the gray-brown of the rock, the patches of moss and the creepers continued on his skin, he became a crouching rumple of clothing, huddled in a pile against the rock.

He saw Jenaro, he saw Jenaro standing just as still as he was, the priest clutching the railing of the bridge he was on, near the end of the arch, his feet still well above the water which reflected him in the light from the fires, fires almost brighter than the sun. The priest had a scream in his eyes, the tears he could let out that Tuscus couldn't no matter how hard he tried, the tears Jen probably didn't notice at all.

He saw Lemeca, behind five of her most trusted workers, all with swords still and makeshift armor from the steel they had forged. He thought, incongruously, that they must be hot under that steel, that the sun could not be treating them kindly and that it must be getting stuffy and smelly under the metal. The armor worked well enough at keeping them protected, though. They did not have to worry about the carapaced ones yet, but there were rebels who decided that they preferred the Sailor's Church after all. There were more and more of those, and they broke their weapons on the armor of the five around Lemeca, not reaching through to her. She called out orders, unobeyed orders, and the shellbacks walked their way to her, taking their time.

Some People Have a Knack for Showing Up at the Most Awkward Time

Then, at his side, Tuscus heard a sigh, and the rock next to him shifted. He turned his head and the bump below his shoulder split itself into a grin, pink gums and light yellow teeth. He saw the granite bumps shift open deep black eyes.

"Such a pity," the voice said from his side.

He could only look at the mouth that moved in the rock.

"You know, Tuscus," it said, "You are going to die. Not eventually, no, but very soon."

"Please, no," Tuscus said, quietly.

The smile and the eyes became a head, a stone head with a scar around a skin flap that covered the bald skull. Then the head shifted color to become a skin tone, but cycled slowly through tanned red to deep black, not deciding on a single one.

"Don't worry, I'm not going to kill you. That's not my job, not what I was assigned to do. I'll even help stop Lemeca from killing you, if she tries. I'm sure she will want to when she gets around to thinking of it. I know I would."

Tuscus recognized the face, he recognized the body encased in what seemed to be stone, fuzzy moss growing over the arms, chest and shins. He saw the man and thought him to be a ghost. Normally he was agnostic on the subject of ghosts and afterlives, but he was leaning toward belief at this point, especially the way the body shifted in his eyesight, visible at one moment, invisible the next, the colors pulsing through it.

"You're dead. I saw you die. You were shot to death and fell in the river."

"No. I'm not dead. I heal very quickly, you know. I'm not at all dead. Not from something like that, especially. I imagine not even someone like you would die from that, though you might if you didn't get enough protein. Protein is very important. Always make sure you eat enough.

"You know, I shouldn't tell you this, but you have had the worst mission I have ever seen in my life. And I didn't even have to help you along much. I mean, I just took this," the letter, the one he had lost so long ago, only four days really, but he felt it to be long, the letter appeared in the rock, then disappeared before he could react. It didn't matter whether it was, really. Tuscus would still claim it was, and that would be the important thing. "And you did the rest. You are a complete fuck-up and it will be a great day when they tear you apart.

The head then said "See, look at that, see, there." And he pointed to where Lemeca was standing with her protectors and the now single carapaced one that bore the mark of the captain, walked toward them, the others hanging back, dispersed into keeping the former rebels, the ones who had turned against Lemeca, away from the five in their steel armor and steel swords. They couldn't break through the steel skin of the guards, but the one shellback, the captain, it strutted under its carapace, if the blank face of the helmet could smile, if the tubes that snaked back from the skull to the rear of the carapace could dance in the wind, if the edge of the visor could lift, they would, but as it was, the curved, hunchbacked form was close to cantering, to dancing.

The guards rushed it, all at once, and it just stood there and let them strike it, and the swords they struck with bent to match the skin of the carapace. Then, it crouched down, it huddled into a ball, and they, crying loudly in triumph under their heavy steel, they struck it again, using what was left of their swords as clubs.

"Now," Fennish said, with all the enthusiasm of one who admires his enemy as much as he hates him, "Watch this. This is what happens when you don't prepare enough, when you get too impatient. This is what will happen if you don't think first and just act. They should know better, but they are too anxious. This is what will happen if you set in motion things you can't control."

The carapace was huddled and the five guards were scrabbling to break it open and then the thing jumped high, throwing off the one on top of him and shocking the others. It fell up and back and fire belched from the arms of the jumper, and the steel melted on the guards bodies and their hair burst into flames and they screamed out of mouths of fire. They scattered like kindling when it landed among them, standing up straight in the flames and pooled metal, and it strolled to Lemeca, who was standing there, open and vulnerable, no chance to defend herself at all. She turned and ran toward the mine.

"Quick, you idiot, fade. I want you to be alive, at least to learn why you will die." And Fennish again became a piece of the mine entrance. Hurriedly, Tuscus did the same. Lemeca rushed past them, deep into the mine, into the elevator, and he heard it descend, scraping the wall as she dropped down too fast, the sparks sounding up the shaft.

"Now do you understand? Do you know why all this, all that," he pointed to the carbon-black bones and metal that had been the guards, to the cluster of ashes that had been those who had been bombed from the dirigible, now simply hovering still, casting a wide shadow on the ground and a group of rebels clustered into a mass, guarded by two of the Church's soldiers, to the Theocratic templars striding about like demons in the remaining fires, "All that is your fault? Now think if you had been on an important mission, one people cared about or trusted you with. How do you think we could trust someone who could single-handedly prevent the Council from having any credibility here for the next hundred years? A man who did for the Church what all their operatives could not have done in a decade? Be thankful that we probably won't be blamed for this, and it will be seen as a natural mistake for you. Your dissection will probably occur after you die, not before. You better make sure they pin none of this on me. Now, I have to stop the mistake from getting bigger still."

And with that, the speaking rock face tippled and brushed past him into the mine, short fast disturbance dropping down the shaft, and Tuscus shifted himself back to his standard color though he couldn't help it if he wanted to, and he understood, and finally, with no relief, he cried.

XXXXVI

Jen's Forced Into Something Else

The massacre was over and Jen was guided off the bridge by the Church's templars. They recognized him as a priest immediately and they guided him to their captain, who was still standing in the midst of their bodies, resting there, leaning back in its shell, in what looked like an awkward pose, but Jen knew it was probably quite comfortable, using the suit for support on his back. It took off its helmet, and he saw a man with a small face, thin lips and wide, joyful eyes.

"Greetings, Father!" he said.

"Brother."

"Sorry, Brother. Tell me, brother, are you the only religious one here?"

"Well, there are a few deacons..." Jen began.

"There always are."

"And there was the parish priest."

"Really? What happened to him?"

"He's over there, on that stake."

Jen gestured to the head. The captain turned to look at it, pursed his lips, looked at it some more, then smiled briefly and turned back to Jen.

"Hmmm. Anyone else?"

Jen pretended to think about it. "Not really, no."

"So, then you are in charge," the captain said.

"No, no I'm not."

"I don't mean of those folk." He gestured to the rebels, "I meant of the loyalists."

"No, I knew what you meant. I have nothing to do with the running of this place."

"Who has been, then? Since he died?" The captain's arm reached back behind him and pointed at the head.

"One of the deacons. She'd been secretary here for..."

"Under your grace, right?"

"Not really."

"Who's been signing papers. You or her? Or someone else?" The captain sounded a bit exasperated to Jen. He'd never known a priest so young and so obviously poor to abdicate responsibility and credit so insistently.

"Well, me. She can't, really."

"Then this was your responsibility?"

"I suppose."

"Ok, then. Father..."

"Brother."

"Brother, right." The captain sighed. "Brother, what should we do with these people?"

"Who, the rebels? I think we should, I don't know, garnish their wages?"

"Garnish their wages?" The captain was incredulous. How, he was thinking, did this boy get through seminary?

"I don't know. Could you give me some time to think?"

"You really need it?" the captain asked.

"I mean, it's not like they didn't have a good reason. I probably would have done what they did. If I was here and I was a different person."

"I don't care what reason they did have. I don't care how good it was. They revolted. They didn't work through the system like everyone else. They got people killed. They've killed themselves. I have no sympathy with whatever their cause was. They should have known better. Just tell me what to do with them."

At this point, Jen happened to glance over to the mine entrance, where he saw a figure crouched down. He stared at it for a while. It seemed like some time to the captain, who was waiting for his answer, but it was more on the order of a few seconds, until it came into focus. He recognized the clothes first, they were still fairly intact, and much cleaner than when he had last saw them, and he saw that the figure was Tuscus. He was hunched over, his head between his knees, his arms wrapped over his shins and pulling his thighs to his chest. This was his first sight of Tuscus since he had left them at the dock two days ago. But Jen recognized the posture, it was one he had seen many times before Tuscus had been taken away from him, and it was one he knew what to do about.

"Well, could you put them some place so I could think about this?"

"Where would like me to put them?"

"I don't know."

"You say that a lot."

"Look, can you put them back to work? Just watch over them and make sure they don't do anything you think might be dangerous."

"You sure?" The captain knew he wasn't.

"Yes. I suppose I am."

"We won't do it. How can we keep an eye on everyone like that? We were only fifteen, but now we're twelve."

"You handled them fine just now," Jen pointed out.

"When they were all in one place. When we could just kill anyone who was attacking us and it was very obvious who was. You think we know enough to deal with any sabotage, even if we were there for it? No, think of something else."

"Well, do you have any ideas?"

"We can't just kill them all," though the captain sounded a bit hopeful at the prospect, especially after talking with Jen for this long.

"No, you can't."

"You have the food to feed them if we locked them up in those buildings there?" the captain pointed to the smelter.

"I don't know. Maybe." Jen looked at Tuscus, curled up, paused, then asked. "Why don't we just let them go home for now?"

"Go home? You crazy? That's just as bad as putting them to work."

"They all live on the other side of the lake. There are already police out over there. They can help keep the peace. At least for a night. I promise I'll tell you what to do with them tomorrow."

"Father...," the captain began, ready to explain to the boy what was wrong with his idea, how it would never work and just would cause more trouble, how he would have to end up fighting house to house and how many more would have to die because of it.

"Brother. Please remember that. Don't go giving me responsibilities I'm not ready for."

"Who is? Never mind, that's another thing altogether. All right, brother, we'll do it. You be ready to tell us what to do tomorrow."

"Yes, captain."

"Brother, I want to..."

"Look, captain, I really have to go." He said it softly, and in a wavering tone, but he was firmer on the matter than the captain guessed, than he would have guessed himself.

"But..." But the captain was speaking to Jen's back as Jen walked over to the mine entrance where Tuscus sat crying.

XXXXVII

Tuscus Confesses

Tuscus looked up and saw Jen coming towards him. He felt both elated and ashamed. Part of him wanted to burrow into the rock, but he did not shift color. It would just reveal what he was to Jen, though Jen had known for some time that this was the case - after all, they had grown up together. He still had enough of a preservation instinct to keep from changing color while someone else, a priest to boot, was watching, so he dug himself against the rock face, so much so that the stone was digging into his skin, cutting him a bit. He buried his head further into his legs, and clung to them so tight his arms went pale.

Jen stood over him, looked straight at the top of his head. He crouched down, hunching on his haunches, and he put his hand on Tuscus' arm and waited there. Time passed, and the captain came over to talk with Jen, but Jen turned his head to look up at the captain, and the captain stared at the two of them, then left. Jen turned to look at Tuscus again, and Tuscus was looking back at him. His eyes avoided Jen's face, while Jen stared intently at his. Jen knew better than to say anything. He knew just to wait, and this is what he did. Tuscus knew he was there, Tuscus wanted did not want Jen to seem him crying. But Jen had seen it before, and Tuscus could not help himself. Jen reached out and held onto Tuscus' arm near his hand, keeping himself a distance.

Jen did not know why he felt as he did while he watched Tuscus cry, but memories of the two of them together came back to him, and memories of everyone since Tuscus. He knew the first would hold a strong pull in his mind, but he still found Tuscus attractive, possibly more so. He knew he did not really know the man anymore, he knew Tuscus might have become all he loathed, but he wanted to think of him as an extension of the beautiful boy he had known, and this weeping Tuscus reinforced that image in his mind. His paternal instinct grew too strong, and Jen leaned forward until he was kneeling close to Tuscus and took the man in his arms. He whispered nonsense to him, he comforted him as best he could, he felt himself fifteen years younger, thirteen again, and under the beds before lights out.

Old habits die hard, for both of them, for then Tuscus told him everything. It was hardly coherent, but Jen found he could decipher it if he didn't pay too much attention. It was in the Council's tongue, of course, the language of their youth, and it was somehow not at all odd to feel the man in his arms ramble like a child. Tuscus told him about Fennish, about his mission, about the envelope, and about his guilt about the revolt. Jen said nothing significant, but he didn't need to.

And then Tuscus was done, and still crying, but less so, and Jen was crying with him too. But then Jen rocked back, and he looked at Tuscus. And Tuscus stopped crying, briefly, and raised his head.

"Who knows that you did this?" Jen asked.

"What do you mean?"

"Please tell me." Tuscus knew the voice Jen was using, it was the one he always used when he was thinking hard. Jen's eyes were looking above Tuscus, at the rock, and Tuscus knew the priest was not just staring idly.

"Well, Fennish. And Lemeca. But I don't think anyone else."

"Are you sure?"

"I can't be."

"But if you had to risk it?" And risk was something taught in seminary. Everyone knew you couldn't make money without risking money. Jen had never liked those lessons, but that was not to say he didn't pay attention.

"I would say those two and maybe the three-eyes. But I think I heard Lemeca tell them that she was in charge."

"Ok, so if those two don't talk to anyone else, then no one knows you made a mistake. As far as your bosses know, you did your job and they went off on their own, despite your protests." Jen had not been sleeping in seminary. He knew what needed to be done, if they could. He knew how to handle a situation like this, something his training, based on selfishness and disloyalty, could deal with more than Tuscus', rooted in adherence to his superiors, could.

"But how would we stop them?"

"They went into the mine, you said?" Jen asked.

"Yes."

"And Fennish was chasing Lemeca?"

"Yes."

"Do you know where she might have gone?"

"I can guess, but I'm not sure."

"One moment." Jen summoned the captain over, and they whispered to each other quickly. The captain called two of his soldiers over, and they stood at either side of the mine's mouth. Jen reached down and took Tuscus' hand. He pulled him gently up.

"Show me." And Jen led him into the mine.

Into the Mine

The two of them, Jen and Tuscus, walked hand in hand into the mine entrance. As they descended in the elevator, Jen held Tuscus' hand carefully, as if it was melting ice, down until they were a mile under the crater of the lake above them. Tuscus related to Jen what had happened the night before, when he had stayed in Lemeca's haven. He spoke to keep himself calm, he spoke because Jen asked him to, but mostly, he told the tale because he couldn't stop talking from sheer nervous energy.

"I've been there before, you know," he started, "Last night, let me tell you, I stayed down here. Jak invited me to go back. I imagine she did the same with you, but I couldn't, you know why, at least now you do, and I needed a place to stay, and Lemeca volunteered this. It was very loud. I couldn't sleep when I wanted to, it was too loud. I had never been this far underground before. You know, that temple in the forest was the deepest I'd ever been, and it is nowhere near as buried as this, and I was quite uncomfortable with that. Not so much the rock above, but more the darkness - everything pitch black, with a uniform temperature, so the only thing I could see was me in those rooms, me and the light bulb, and that only until it cooled, the door was sealed so tight. So I laid awake for a bit, and ended up turning on the lamp. I dressed again, and I walked out and around.

"Now, normally, I could not do that, not at home, but there I knew where everything was that I needed to know about, and what I didn't, my Administrator had blocked off clearly. But last night, (wow, we aren't even a quarter of the way down, I didn't know this trip was so long) I didn't know anything. I followed the noise down to a hall filled with people. And let me tell you, they were celebrating.

"The hall was covered in food, the walls were smeared from people throwing it at each other, the tables were just bursting. And there were people everywhere. They were singing, loudly, all different songs. In the middle of it was Lemeca. She was walking around, checking on them all, you know? And she was very happy. I could tell. There was this stage there, and she would jump on it and dance for a bit, and people would clap and cheer here when she did. I sat down at one of the farther tables, and I ate some of the food. It was quite good. They had these fruit things in this caramel sauce. No, I didn't get the recipe. I still can't cook. After a bit, it got even louder, mostly because people who I had thought left to go to sleep or things came back with instruments, and they started to play. They really weren't that good. I think they didn't know which song to play, but they stuck to the beat of this guy with a drum (he was good, and loud, but I think more loud than good. It helped everyone was keeping up with him and not anyone else) and soon Lemeca had dragged quite a few people onto the stage, and people were falling off it.

"About that time, she saw me. She tried to get me to dance with her, but you know I can't dance. Also, I was covered in the juice and sauce, and they were both sticky and I didn't feel like touching anyone at that point. Remember you asked me how I knew only her and Fennish knew what had happened? Because right after I turned her down, she stood on a table, and she toasted me (I think she was toasted herself by this point) and she said that I was the one who had helped her dream come to pass, but that it would have happened without me, but she was glad to have me anywise, even if I was useless. Now, I was mad when she said it. I was very mad, but then, it's for the best, I suppose. After all, it means no one will blame this on me, if Fennish doesn't tell anyone. Lemeca can't blame me for anything without making herself look like a liar, and I don't think she would do that. Well, she might. I don't know her that well.

"But I sat there for a while and watched them carry on, and they did carry on. I didn't get drunk enough to really enjoy what was happening, just enough to get tired again, and just enough so I could get to sleep what with the noise from the party. It worked well enough, and I was able to get to sleep, but it took probably another hour. Oh, look, here we are."

Tuscus opened the door of the elevator. The shaft wall was

before them, not an inch from the door, and Jen was sure that Tuscus had made a mistake, but he pushed on the wall, frowned, shifted his hand, pushed again, said "Give me a moment, I only saw people do this maybe three times. I'm sure this is the right spot, though." He tried a few more spots before the shaft opened into a hallway. He stepped across the gap between the elevator and the floor of the hall and Jen followed, looking down but seeing nothing interesting, as it was all black.

Tuscus did seem much happier to Jen, his babble on the way down proved this to him. Perhaps, Jen thought, it was the hope that he will live after all. Jen knew that spies were one of the few people in the Council programmed with what the Administrators would view as an enhanced survival instinct. Spies with a sense of self-preservation were more likely to return with information and not get caught. On the other hand, Jen's fellow students in seminary had noticed that he seemed to be lacking in one, at least one on par with their own. His distinct lack of greed proved that to them. Of course, they didn't mention any of that to Jen, those who liked him not wanting to hurt him and those who hated him not wanting to point out a flaw they might exploit.

They walked into a bare rock hall, lit from parallel strips of light along the walls, and Tuscus continued.

"Now, I was woken up by Lemeca, so I didn't get to find out where she was sleeping, which might help us find her, but maybe not. I'm pretty sure she came down here, though. There is nowhere else she can hide, I'm pretty sure. But who knows? She was a smart woman in some ways, she might have other places in the mine. But this is the best bet, I think. Want to see the banquet hall? Completely pointless, I thought, but it helped them rally, and I think maybe that counts for something. Through those doors there."

They opened the double doors to the banquet hall that Tuscus had eaten in the night before. The light was dim, except for the spotlight onto the stage. All the doors were closed and were letting in no air and no light, only the door Jen and Tuscus were standing in was letting any in. The tables were laid out as if they were simply awaiting the guests before the meal could begin. The utensils were in the bowls, the plates and cups were empty and upside-down to keep dust away, the face cloths and hand towels were soaking in bowls of water. The chairs were snug against the table, and waitcarts were at every intersection, bottles of all descriptions and large slabs of roast sitting on them, the roast covered with gauze soaked in marinade which was still dripping along its skin. It seemed as if the room was waiting to be used and a throng would come through at any moment, ready to listen to speeches, then get drunk and singing late into the night in triumph.

But on closer inspection, it was clear it all had been sitting there for over an hour, the ice had melted in the carafes, the vegetables were starting to droop, and water was spreading in damp circles from beneath the bowls. The water the hand and face cloths were soaking in was foggy from collapsed soap bubbles.

Jen and Tuscus did not notice any of this. As should be the case, the stage held their attention, on it, a spotlight tight around a figure, immobile, on the stage. And that figure they had their eyes drawn to was Lemeca, and she was not moving, hanging from strings tied at her elbows and wrists and knees and feet. She was dangling, half-face down, half-facing the main entrance, and she was not moving, not struggling. The floor beneath her was perfectly clean, as if she had not even stepped on it, as if it had been scrubbed for the to see herself, though her head was lolled back and looking, with a tilt, at the door, and the floor reflected her body to the ceiling, which wasn't paying attention. It reflected that her skin was hanging open and inside she was red and empty, and though blood rolled down her legs and arms, not one drop fell to the floor to mar its perfect mirror.

Jen sat down in one of the chairs, and Jen stood behind him, holding it. Neither of them really knew Lemeca, Jen had just seen her from a distance, but it was a shock to come across her like that, especially since they were expecting to have to chase her down. It was also the second mutilated corpse, not to mention the god in the temple and its paladin, or the three-eye whose throat he'd ripped out, Jen had seen in as many days, and he wasn't liking it the more he was exposed to the sight. He began to wonder if there was something wrong with him, with all the bodies that were starting to crop up around him.

Tuscus was nowhere near as disturbed, though he knew Lemeca a little. He just needed to think of her like the anatomy classes he had taken, where nonsapients, who were human in all other respects, were dissected in class. The more he thought of her that way, the more he noticed how close it was to what he was seeing. The cuts in the skin were a one-to-one correspondence with those incisions, and the spread skin was perfectly hung to clearly display the inside with no obstruction.

The more he looked, the more he realized the cuts were made with an eye to curiosity and efficiency more than anything else.

"Well, that takes care of one of them," Tuscus said with a sigh.

"Do you know who did this?"

"I couldn't tell you. Maybe someone mad about how the revolt turned out? It doesn't matter anyway. She's dead, after all. It's not like we weren't going to do the same thing to her anyway. Well, maybe not exactly the same thing."

"You realize, that if it is because of the revolt, they might come after you."

Tuscus shook his head. "No, I don't think that will happen. I told you, she took all the credit."

"Did anyone believe her? Did anyone notice that not even one day had passed between when you showed up and when the revolt started?"

"What if they did? By the time anyone saw me, they would have been too drunk to remember me."

Jen didn't know what to say to that. He thought the boy was being naive, but he didn't want to say so.

"Wait a minute before you feel safe, ok? You said Fennish went in here right before we did."

"Well, not right before. Maybe half an hour, maybe longer."

"But still, he came down here, but would he have know where she would have been? I don't think he could have found that out so quick. I hope not. What if he is still here, what if he's watching us? What if he's waiting to kill us?"

"What for?" Tuscus asked. "He said he wouldn't kill me.

He told me that he'd let my superiors do that after they've judged me as best they could."

"He didn't say he that about me. What if he wants to kill me? Could you protect me? Would you?"

"Of course I would." Tuscus said. "Don't be silly."

"I'm worried. Let's leave."

"Look, nothing will happen if it hasn't already. I think Fennish could care less about you. Why should he waste his energy like that?"

"Because I know about the both of you. He could kill me for that. How do we know that she didn't die for the same reason?"

"You're a priest. If you died, there would be an investigation. He wouldn't want that. This was one thing we were always taught, never to assassinate anyone of the priesthood, unless necessary. You people don't care about the lay folk, but when one of your own is killed, no stream is unfollowed."

"How can you say that, when your own government..."

Tuscus interrupted. "It was once yours."

"Your own government, not mine, kills its own people for education, or if they don't wake up on time, or if they get in the way, or if they start to eat too much or too little."

"But those people aren't sapients," Tuscus protested.

"How do you know? Did you see their souls? What about you, you're going to die if Fennish gets back to your country before you do and tells that what's happened."

"But I deserve to."

"Why? Because you failed?"

"Yes. I failed spectacularly. Do you need any more reason?

Why should I take resources away from those who are more competent than me? Why should they be punished?"

Jen sighed. "Never mind. I don't think we're going to get anywhere with this."

"And why should I have to live knowing how I failed. I would love the mercy of being killed so I don't have to live every day for a hundred years, or more, knowing that I caused those people up there to die and my country to lose its chance of gaining that land, possibly forever."

"So why don't you kill yourself then?"

"I can't. I'm programmed not to." Tuscus paused, his head hanging. "I'm made to be too scared."

"You always were. Remember? And you became the spy."

"That was what I was designed for. How could I refuse?"

"Well, I wasn't designed to be a priest, I know that."

"Really?" Tuscus said, obviously being sarcastic.

"So what would I have been? What have you found that could be me?"

"I don't know. Not a priest or a merchant. That much is obvious."

Now, Jen had thought he had hidden his lack of avarice fairly well. This was something that he had worked on for years (it could have killed his career as a priest, after all) and he thought he had hid it successfully. Everyone knew, but they were too polite to say anything, especially with the way he could accumulate wealth so quickly that it embarrassed him. But to have the absence of greed so clear that Tuscus could tell it threw him. He was shattered that his deception had been uncovered. Tuscus was basing his statement on Jen's behavior as a child, he couldn't guess either way whether Jen had grown greedy in the fifteen years since they had parted. He suspected not, but he couldn't know for sure.

"What do you mean by that?" Jen asked.

"Just that you are not designed for this job."

"Do you doubt me as a priest?"

"I'm sure you're sincere. I'm sure they've brainwashed you into believing you make a great priest."

"Brainwashed? How can you, of all people, say that I was brainwashed?"

"Well, I wasn't. I'm the same as I was. You're the one who threw away your childhood for this new country of yours, one that destroyed your history, our history."

"You're the one who wants to kill yourself over nothing."

"Nothing? Did you see how many people died because of me?"

"If you kill yourself, that will just be one more."

"But no one else will die because of me. That will be the last of it."

"How do you know that? How do you know you didn't save more lives than were lost?" Jen asked.

"I can't. But that's a silly metric. I can't judge on potential, just on what happened."

"You'll never know."

"I do. I know I failed."

Jen threw up his hands. "It always comes back to that with you."

"It is all there is left to me."

"That's not true."

"Yes, it is."

"So, why should we find Fennish, if you want to die and he's not going to kill me?" Jen asked, angrily.

"I don't know. Because I don't want to be alive when they dissect me, because if I turn myself in, and he doesn't say anything, I will die painlessly."

"Rubbish. Your survival instinct is well coded. It runs deeper than you think. You want him gone because you won't turn yourself in..."

"I will." Tuscus said, offended.

"You won't turn yourself in, you'll make it all out to be her," Jen couldn't refer to the corpse directly, still, though he had almost forgotten it as they argued, though his eyes were still on the body hanging over the floor and he imagined it was starting to turn a little. "And when you do, you will be blameless, you will have told her not to do this, but you'll say that she ignored you."

"I won't."

"Yes, you will. You will then blame it on cowardice, and hate yourself, but like the Church teaches, most times cowardice is simply wisdom disguised."

"How can you say that about me?"

"Because you're smarter than you think, than you know, and you know that that will be the right decision."

Tuscus' voice turned bitter. "Is this how you comfort the masses, father?"

"Brother. I suppose so. I've not really done it much. This is my first."

"Well, you aren't doing a good job."

"Are you going to turn yourself in?"

"Of course."

"You're going to tell the truth until you're lying on the dissection table."

"So be it."

"All right, if that's it, then good-bye." Jen rose and started walking to the door.

"Wait. Where are you going?"

"I'm not going to help you commit suicide. I don't believe in suicide, especially not something as ridiculous as martyrdom. That's one of those things I was brainwashed into believing in seminary, by the way."

"Come back."

"No."

"Jen, come back! Come back!" But Jen was out the door

Jak Tries to Make The Trip
Less of a Total Loss

Back on the surface, Jak was yelling at the captain's lieutenant. In part, she was yelling because he was on the shore and she was on her barge, but she probably would have been doing so if he had been next to her. Her husband was tugging at her, trying to get her to lower her voice, but this only served to annoy her further, which she took out on the lieutenant, who responded to her loudly, but only so as to be heard.

"I won't get anything for this?" she was shouting.

"I'm sorry, but..."

"You're sorry, my ass."

"Captain..." the lieutenant pleaded.

"What? You are going to tell me what? It better be good, you asshole."

"You should be thankful to have helped your government."

"What? Help my government? You think I care about that? Why should I?"

"You came to get us, didn't you?"

"I came for the money," Jak lied.

"Is money all you cared about?"

"Yes! I want it now!"

"I'm sorry, captain. We have no money to give you."

At this point, Jak's husband talked to her quietly, while she was gathering her breath.

"Dear," he said.

"What?" she snapped.

"One moment, please."

"Ok," She shouted toward the shore. "You stay there. I have more to say to you. Or you can give my money."

"I don't have any."

"What do you mean you don't have..."

Jak's husband tugged at her. "Dear."

"Right. You wait." She turned to her husband. "What?"

"You like that word a lot today."

"You don't make me madder."

"Sorry. You didn't tell me about any money."

"I didn't."

"You were hiding that from me?"

"I wouldn't do that. You know that."

"You weren't expecting anything."

"Don't say that so loud. Of course not." She smirked.

"Then why are you being so mercenary?" he asked.

"We went out of our way, right? What would happen if we

didn't get anything out of it?"

"I don't know. You handle all that sort of thing."

"I'll tell you. We might have earned a little favor or two, but the whole thing is a loss, financially."

"They gave us fuel and food. It didn't cost us supplies."

"Breaking even is the same as losing. Remember that, ok?"

"Everything living has to grow or die." They said simultaneously.

He sighed. "Yes, yes, I know. But we brought them out of goodwill."

"You want them to know that? You think they'll respect us for it? How will we look, giving free rides to the Church?"

"Fairly good, I should think."

"Think of it this way...would the Church do the same?"

"Well, no, but..."

"Has the Church ever done anything out of altruism?"

"Well, they..."

"Everything they did, they profited from, either in hard capital or in goodwill. If you read or hear about how the Church has helped, oh, I don't know, someone who was impoverished by fire, you feel good about the church, right? You think better of them, right? You would be more likely to do what they Church asked you and question them less, right? So they came out of the situation with a profit, and a damned big one at that."

Her husband had been nodding along, but after that, he was perplexed.

"Come on, I'm not spelling everything out for you. If you didn't learn this already, just from being alive, or you can't see how the Church's charity makes money in buckets.... They won't respect us if we don't show them how we follow the same principles. Now we could care less about the public's goodwill."

"We have no public."

"Right," Jak said, encouragingly.

"We do, though, we do. Our customers, what about them? And..."

"They're not important right now. We need to go after the Church's goodwill. That means getting their respect. That means trying to gouge them out of as much as we can because that is what they would do to us."

He stirred the water with his hand. "I understand."

"Will you help?"

"Of course, dear."

"Good," she raised her voice. "Hey, I didn't tell you to go away."

"You were..."

"I have to come over there?"

"Why, yes."

"You better have a sack of cash for me."

"I told you..."

"Or get your captain out here and have him pay me."

"I can't do that," the lieutenant said.

"Hubby mine, start up the barge and bring out the knives."

"You don't have to..."

The barge moved slowly to the shore.

"You really want to be on the shore? I've killed many young men in my time. Killing you won't bother me at all."

"Captain, please calm down," he pleaded.

"You want to fight me for my hard-earned money or are you going to get your captain and give me what I deserve?"

"I suppose I can do that."

"And he better be bringing my pay with him."

L

Fennish Meets the Boys

Fennish knew that he needed to stay in the depths of the earth. He knew he could hide in plain sight, if he wanted, but he wanted to rest for a while. He was hungry and tired, he had exercised too much recently, and he wasn't used to the exertion. Lemeca's organs and muscle had fed him some, but it only went so far. Running from the eyes of the priest had taken a lot out of him. It was almost as if the priest was really blessed by his god, coming so close to finding him so many times, simply by accident. He didn't even have the energy to try to follow Tuscus. He didn't want to risk his life on the guess that no one would notice him. One thing that had worked towards his favor was his stumbling on Lemeca's storerooms, and he holed himself in, barricaded the door, and recovered.

He wasn't too proud of himself. The boy had seen Lemeca,

and he must be scared for his life. It was one thing if the threat was abstract, just talk about his demise, but the boy had seen what had happened to Lemeca, and that, combined with the threat, must have given him a more clear understanding of what truly lay ahead of him if he returned to the Oligarchy. Fennish knew very well that people were more than willing to sacrifice themselves to a cause if they could not conceive of what the sacrifice truly entailed. Martyrdom is a welcome choice to those who don't understand the finality, especially not the sort that Tuscus had just been exposed to as he looked upon Lemeca's properly dissected carcass. Fennish knew he had his work cut out for him to get the boy back where he belonged.

It made no difference if he stayed in the mine, Fennish rationalized. After all, Tuscus would follow Jen wherever the priest went. Jen was the only one the boy knew, really, especially in this country. Jen had been Tuscus' obsession to the point of excluding any but the most fleeting of friendships. The boy would stay around the priest. He knew the priest was stuck in town, he knew the priest would go back to Nephi to report to the bishop, and he simply needed to be there before the two of them arrived. The best bet would be to catch Tuscus as he entered the town of Nephi and spirit him away while Jen was with the bishop. There would be little protest, if any, if the bishop didn't thank him for getting her out of an awkward spot. No one would notice them, if he did it quietly enough.

Jen did not know where he was going when he left the banquet hall. He almost found his way back to the elevator, but he could not remember the route fully. He had not been concentrating on learning his way when he walked in. He hadn't been expecting to leave without Tuscus. And so, he took the wrong turn, almost immediately, but the rest of his navigation would have been right, if he had been correct at first.

The halls were unlit, but brightened when he stepped into the rooms and corridors. His eyes were constantly adjusting to the change in light level, and he started seeing ghosts around objects in his sight. They would pass in front of his eyes and he could not find his way, so he followed them, and his eyes were tearing with the strain. He thought he saw Tuscus, more than once, and Fennish several other times. He actually did, not every time, but often enough to suggest them in the changing light, his eyes shifting the white noise into images it could handle as they were leaving the room, running through, seeming to chase each other.

The rooms themselves were nondescript, after the first. They were lined with slits along the ceiling, they were lined with slits along the floor. The rock had been smoothed and whitewashed, the floor was slick from polishing, with sweeps of rock carved out from the polishers arcing their strokes. In the rooms, there were crates, a common feature in Jen's life by this point. He tried to pry a few open, but could not, and so gave up. Chairs and books were scattered around the crates, as if there had been people there watching them but they had just left for a moment, perhaps to retire to the bathroom or grab a bite to eat, but they held no interest to him, he was too disoriented to read, to sit down long enough for them. His eyes hurt too much.

Tuscus was sitting in the dark. He had returned to the room Lemeca was hanging in after performing a cursory search. He reasoned that he could not leave Jen alone in the mine, it would not be responsible of him, since he blamed himself for leading Jen down the shaft in the first place. He figured that if he stayed in one place, he was more likely to have Jen run across him then if he moved about hunting him. It was a tactic he had been taught when he was in the nursery, and he had never thought about how it wouldn't work if everyone was staying still. He had disabled the elevator by removing the lever that controlled its movement. He held the lever in the hand he kept closest to Lemeca's corpse, protecting himself from it and the sight of it. He entertained himself, briefly, by hunting for the lights, but he could not figure out the controls he found, and so he gave up after playing with them and creating no real change. He also started to snack on the food left on the tables, until he realized it was starting to spoil, and he gave up on it.

He pulled a table in front of the stage, snug against it, and climbed up on it, facing away from the corpse, his body illuminated, outlined by the light behind him, casting a long shadow before him, and he watched the doors, waiting for Jen to return.

Fennish saw the priest ahead of him, blindly coming his way. He had been avoiding the boy for some time, yet Jen always seemed to hunt him down, actually catching him on several occasions but never seeming to notice. But this time, Fennish had nowhere to go but the main hall, where he had left Lemeca's body hanging on hooks. He had thought that it was nicely artistic, a beautiful touch, when he done it the first time, but he was beginning to regret the decision the more he thought of it.

Perhaps he should have burned her, or sent her up the elevator to the Theocracy's troops. They would have been happy to have her and would ignore the other implications of finding her, but he berated himself for the drive to perfection he had, and how his desire to finally hang someone up on a stage had worked out. She did provide enough nutrients, almost, but he still hadn't had the time to rest and process them. He supposed he could have left most of her behind and not gorged himself, just enough to keep questions from being asked, but he had been so hungry.

The priest was still coming towards him, and he could go nowhere. The walls, so plain, the floor, so empty, and this place, the one he was standing in, was the first without the clutter of books and crates and tools that the others had had. Though he could only match the walls and floor, he stood still and changed himself until he became the wall, until he was unable to be seen, his skin was the same off-white as the area around him, and he closed his eyes, hoping that the priest had not seen him yet, and held his breath.

The priest's footsteps stopped, close to him, and he knew better than to move. Perhaps Jen had seen his outline. There was very little he could do about that, though he had had years of practice, but no mimicry, especially not one done as quickly as this, could be perfect, and the plain white of the hall did nothing to break up the line of distortion. He did not stand out as much as Jen's dark reddish-brown, but this was little consolation, the priest was hardly tying to hide. He stood still, hoping that Jen would pass him by and attribute the outline to a trick of the light.

The priest came closer and closer, Fennish could feel his breath on every part of his skin, especially his face, and the priest was loud, his clothes rustling over each other, his breathing a raspy howl in the white, plain corridor, and Fennish was starting to feel faint, though he'd only been holding his breath for a minute.

He wished he could kill the priest, his hunger was starting to rise in him, but he couldn't, he'd been ordered not to, not to cause any suspicion, not any more, and the death of a priest would do just that. Even though his hunger was starting to be so strong, almost as strong as it had been when he had killed Lemeca, he had orders, and he, like Tuscus, had no choice when it came to orders. He knew that disobeying was a sure death, more so than anything else. Wasn't it his duty to escort Tuscus to die for the same reason? But his breath was getting stale, too early for him, normally, and his bursting stomach was screaming for more.

"You know, Fennish," the priest said, "You really should wipe your mouth after you eat someone."

Jen stepped back from the hovering mouth, outlined in dried blood, invisible from the back, but holding itself there in the air, closed tight in a flat line, amidst a barely visible distortion the shape of a short, bald man. The mouth stood still, not moving at all, steady in the middle of the corridor.

"Fennish, you aren't fooling anyone."

The mouth opened slightly, but only slightly, and breathed.

"Someone had to kill Lemeca, and I'm glad it was you

and not me. I really can't stand that sort of stuff, and death has been too much a part of my life recently. I really don't like to see it. I can't imagine how you and Tuscus must live with yourselves, both of you killing so much. Still, you won't kill each other. And one of you has to, if either of you are going to go back home. I tell you, Tuscus won't go back on his own now, you would call him a coward for not doing his duty, but I think that it only makes sense. Why die if you don't have to? But he wants to go back, and not for execution. It is his home, right? So that means that there can be no evidence that he caused all this. You are the only one who knows what he did, at least from the Council, and I can't ask you to lie on his behalf.

"You wouldn't do that, would you? You are too loyal, you do your job, just as you should. You have to, that's the way you and Tuscus were designed. And the way I was too, because, after all, I was born in the same nursery as Tuscus, in the Oligarchy, and I got the same base geneset that everyone else there did. And that means that I have to do my job, as a priest of the Sailor, and part of my job is to make myself richer. If Tuscus lives, I am richer, for I have him, or at least the potential of him. If he dies, I am poorer. Much poorer. So I have to do my duty. To myself, to my friend, to the priesthood. I have to kill you."

Two eyes appeared above the mouth, eyes full of lust and starvation, two nostril holes sprung open. and they hung together there, static. Then, a blur, and Jen fell down, his eyes unseeing, and left alone in the hall.

LI

Offices Should Not Be Built to Be Slept In

Jen sat at the desk, his head resting on it, buried under his arms. Tuscus slept on the floor beside the desk, on his side, curled up, not even feeling the hardness of the floor, just dreaming. The door opened, the secretary looked in, and she smiled, placed the key to the monk cells in the basement on the floor wrapped in a kerchief, and she shut the door behind her as she left the office.

Jen and Tuscus slept there for some time, near each other, with the window showing the lights of the town wink out one by one, until there was no light left save the water reflected lamps of the police as they wandered about the town. An hour later, with Cain in the sky, just reaching over the temple and visible through the window, the planetlight disturbed them and they both woke up.

The giant hung over the water, brighter than they normally

saw it, in more populated climes, in regions where the day and the night were equally bright. In fact, those who were working in Semt were seeing it as if for the first time as well, as the foundry was idle that night as it hadn't been as long as a mine had been in the town, and the red flare from the ground did not drown out the planet's light. Its reflection was a broken trail of light on the water, reaching up to touch the great eye of the window, the bands of clouds that were so visible on the surface of the giant in the sky were smeared into a light pink on the water, the thin line of its ring not visible, not even as a thin divider in the sky. There were no buildings in the way, on the water, the shore the only impediment to the light, and it was there, at the green, black in this light, of the shore grasses that the light broke off.

When Jen woke up, he saw Cain hanging in the window, a bright circle in the black, the pupil of an eye inverted. He looked up at it, lost in thought, no particular ones, just random bustle of white noise that ended up equating itself with nothing, the same thoughts that everyone raised on a moon (or a planet with an outsized moon) has when there stare up at the companion body. He heard Tuscus stir, and he was surprised to hear that the man had stayed in his office, sleeping on the floor while he slouched in his chair. He did not notice the drool he had left behind on the desk's otherwise clean finish, even though he put his elbow in it as he leaned to look out the window.

"Good night," he said.

"Mmmm," Tuscus responded, "Damn, my neck."

"Is it ok?"

"I think so, I think so, let me check." Tuscus rolled his

head around quickly, three times one way and three the other. "Ouch, no."

"Here, come here."

"Ok." Tuscus scooted so that his back was to Jen, at the base of the chair, and they both looked out the window into the black and the rippling light.

"Here, let me try this." Jen put his hands on Tuscus' neck. Tuscus flinched, and the priest withdrew his hands.

"What's the matter?"

"It's just that, well, you were never very good at that."

"It's been fifteen years, give me a chance, ok?"

"Have you practiced?" Tuscus asked, teasing as best he could with his sore neck.

"Of course, I always remembered you howling and begging me to stop."

"You're exaggerating."

"Not by much."

"Let me try again, ok?"

In response, Tuscus grabbed Jen's hands and placed them on his neck. Jen started kneading, and slowly tried to tease the muscles out of tension. Tuscus' muscles just grew more and more tense as Jen worked away at them.

"Ow! Damn! Stop, stop!"

"Ok, sorry."

"I think you just made it worse."

"Sorry, sorry, I didn't mean it."

"Oh, don't worry, I don't think it's you, I think it's me, I never have liked that sort of thing."

"Are you sure?"

"Of course," Tuscus lied, but Jen didn't know better.

"Ok, what should I do?"

"I don't know, just distract me, I guess."

"How?"

Tuscus' mind raced at the question, as did Jen's, but neither of them wanted to say what they both were thinking.

"Just talk to me, ok?" Tuscus asked.

"About what?"

"I don't know."

"You know, you've been avoiding telling me what happened in the mine."

"I know."

"Why?" Jen asked.

"I'm not too proud of it."

"Well, I'm not going to blame you for anything. After all, I'm still alive."

"You were never in any danger. Fennish could not kill either of us. He'd been ordered not to."

"How do you know?" Jen asked.

"Because he brought you to me, when you were unconscious. I never would have found you otherwise. I was waiting for you to come back, you know."

"Maybe he wanted to kill us together."

"I don't think so. He would have killed and eaten you, like he did Lemeca, if he could have. After all, you knew everything he didn't want to get out, and if he could quiet you and me at the same time, then that is what would have happened. He would have done the same to me long ago, but he told me straight out he couldn't. I told you that. And when he brought you in, I knew that the same applied to you. And then I knew he couldn't threaten me with your death. And that was important."

"You're sweet," Jen said, half seriously.

Tuscus was glad that Jen couldn't see his skin redden in the Cainlight.

"And when I knew that, I also knew that I could kill him. You see, he had to deliver me to the dissection table. So I killed him."

"How?"

"How does anyone kill anyone else? I'll tell you this, I tried to be as clean about it as he was with Lemeca. The less evidence, the better."

"What happened to his body? Did you bring it up with you?" Jen asked.

"I burned it. Remember, I do work for your enemy, I don't want them to find any trace of Fennish. When I go back, I have to be the only evidence of what really happened. It's better for everyone that way."

"You're not practicing lying to me, are you? Is that what really happened?"

"It might as well be." He remembered his deep weakness and his deep, driving, need for energy, any sort, as he looked at Fennish and his broken neck and felt his own blood pour out from his side. He remembered taking Fennish's empty skin, gray-brown with a red-brown patch on the back of the head, in the humming light, and bundling it in Lemeca's and casting them both down the mine shaft. He remembered frantically cleaning the elevator lever as he and the unconscious Jen rode up to the surface. "Please, just talk to me, but not about anything important."

And they talked, until Cain set and the city was black again. They left the office then, and found the keys on the floor, and they retired together to the monk's cell that Jen had been staying in. Though the only bed was small, the blanket was easily big enough for both of them.

When they woke up in the morning, they both were warmer than they were used to, and Jen had a cramp in his arm to match the one in Tuscus' neck that hadn't gone away, from where he had held it all night above Tuscus' head. But he was happier still than he had been in some time, though he was running on little sleep. Jen looked over to Tuscus, and wondered if he could kiss the man yet, what the etiquette was.

He didn't want to seem to forward, though he knew that it was ridiculous to speculate that revulsion would be Tuscus' response. But then, perhaps, he thought, Tuscus had slept with him as a friend only, and nothing more, as nothing had really happened beyond talk and sleep and chaste hugs. Of course, at the same, time, Tuscus was thinking the exact same things, and they both just looked at each other a bit before rolling out of the bed.

When Jen and Tuscus opened the door to the priest's antechamber, the secretary was there with the captain of the templars. They were waiting, and they looked at the two of them with slight smiles that they hid quickly. Jen nodded and made his way to the office door, but the captain stood in front of it fairly firmly. Jen stopped, and Tuscus slipped back to the side of the entrance door, his skin starting to match the wall texture before he noticed the changing and stopped it.

"Hello, Jen," the secretary said.

"Good morning. Why won't he let me in?"

"You're not needed here anymore."

"Really?" Jen did his best not to sound eager, but it wasn't as difficult as he had expected. He found some desire to be on the other side of the door, signing his name to documents he was just beginning to understand. He wanted Tuscus with him, helping him work through the convoluted wordings, he wanted to explain to Tuscus how, for example, increasing worker's salaries across the board would just make their money worth that much less.

"The bishop wants you back in Nephi as soon as possible," the secretary said.

"Was there any indication why?"

"She wants your report. From your mission."

"Which mission?"

"How should I know? No one told me anything about it." The secretary shrugged. "I'll miss you, maybe. I think you would have done a good job here, better than the last few at least, even if it has only been a few days. I can tell the difference. You always this conscientious?"

"Well, most of the time, I try, but ... That's neither here nor there. How did you get these orders? We don't have a radio. Do we?"

"We don't."

The captain spoke, "We sent the dirigible to the bishop yesterday morning, after we were sure you could handle anything that could happen in the course of a day. It came back last night. The bishop wants your report to her now."

As they started to leave, Jen saw the secretary reach into her desk and pull out a skull that had recently been scraped clean.

"Don't worry," she said, "It's not for you. Now, get along." She shooed them away.

Jen opened the door, and behind it, Brother Tubret stood, trying to be somber but not succeeding very well. When he saw Jen and Tuscus, his face darkened and he smiled tightly at them. He stepped through the opened door, not bothering to wait to talk to the boys, and they heard the secretary say "Catch," as she threw the skull at him.

LII

High Resolution

The day that they left Semt was unique in only one way. It was one of those days were everything was in high resolution, as if the world had just remembered color and all the other days were gray next to it. It was one of those days where Jen did not want to stop looking at anything, did not want to blink, and everything was more real than it had ever been. As if he had stepped through into the real world for a moment, one he knew would not last.

But he stood on the barge as it trundled down the river, the short way to where the dirigible was moored, and he saw Cain in the sky, near Nod. The next day would be the beginning of the next week, but as it stood, Cain was a large incoherent mass following the sun. The forest was as quiet as always at this time of the day. There were no small animals rustling except the rats and the roaches that followed humanity wherever it went.

The dirigible's screw was already turning, idling really, but the faster propeller was sweeping around every minute, the slower at half that speed. It was pulling on the guy ropes, but not too strongly, and the tri-lobed black bag that held the supporting gas was gleaming in the morning sun, almost swelling under their gaze as the sun heated up the gas within it. The pilot was looking out at the river, and he waved to them when he saw them, quite enthusiastically. Even so, it took some time for them to catch him, and they waved up at him as the barge was tied up.

Tuscus scrambled up the mooring mast so fast that he seemed to float up to the dirigible. He waited for the plank into the gondola to be lowered, but only barely. Even so, Jen, who climbed much slower, was at the top, standing next to him by the time it came down. Tuscus climbed over, followed by Jen, who stood on the plank, over the empty air and the river below, between the floating gondola and the tall, spindly, wooden mast, looking down onto the barge. He shouted good-bye, and the people on it, already untying themselves, looked up, but did not call back. Jen waited a little bit, but then walked into the gondola and helped the pilot pull up the plank and stow it before he settled into the exquisitely carved chairs that were spaced about the plush red-carpeted gondola.

In the air, over the forest, near the river, columns of smoke strung up into the air. It was all coming in a line pointing to a clearing, a clearing with what looked like a crumple of rock as its center. Jen stared at it, trying to make out the image before him, but he could not recognize the pile of rubble from the air. As they drew closer, drifting over the river, he still couldn't see the clearing well, but the dirigible passed close to one of the smoke trails, and Jen looked down.

He saw, around and beneath him, tall, naked bald people, fighting carapaced warriors, neither seeming to make much progress against the other. When he shifted his gaze to the next, deeper in the forest, though not as visible, he saw the same thing. And so he leapfrogged from one cloud to the other, all of the sites of smoke the same, silent to him except for the turning of the screw propelling the dirigible, both dynamic in their energy but static as none of them were close to any outcome.

He looked again to the clearing as it slipped behind him, and he saw the glint of refracted light and wooden huts around the rock, which he recognized as the ruin of the temple, its cold blue light extinguished by the sun, crawling with soldiers and fire. He tapped Tuscus' arm, and pointed out to the rubble. They both looked out to it until the scene slipped out of sight.

LIII

Rainy Season

Jen's report to the bishop was concise, but left out nothing. He had been telling the truth to Fennish when he said that duty had been bred into him. The verbal report glossed over most of the details, but the written one was a ream of paper in and of itself, much more than the bishop wanted, and she passed it off to one of her more dependable priests who had a hunger for such things. Jen didn't see Tuscus for the month he wrote the text, except briefly, when Tuscus would show up at his cell, demanding his company.

But then, when the report was in, and Tuscus had left to the Oligarchy and returned, without Jen's noticing that he was gone for a week and a half, they began to see more of each other. Tuscus told Jen that that was his assignment, to spy on Jen and the other parish priests, a fact Jen dutifully told the bishop, as Tuscus knew he would. But the rains were coming, and everything was winding up for the year, the boats, except those that were absolutely necessary, were covered, the windows were reinforced, the lower floors sealed against the soon rising waters, and no one would care until the next year, when the rain stopped.

And the Ship, high in its orbit, lanced a beam down into the waters of the widest ocean, energy it had been collecting for a full year, and that beam burned through the sky, turning it into arcing plasma conduit, white and writhing, smelling of ozone. If anyone could get so close to see it, and a few of the more fanatic did so each year, it would be their last act. That beam boiled the water, rolls of steam rising into the humid air, collecting into clouds, thickening clouds, that spread out from the beam at half the speed of sound, creeping over the globe and enveloping it, the beam pumped energy into the water until the clouds blocked it, diffracted it into a brilliant spread of light.

The rainy season was starting, Jen knew this as he stared out the window. The sun had been getting dimmer. The traditional start of the rainy season, a star high in the sky near the sun, had been seen earlier that day, so Jen knew it was going to be raining, and soon. A flicker then a flare of spectra ran through the sky, under spreading clouds. With Tuscus in hand, he walked out onto the roof of the cathedral, above the cell the bishop had appointed to him.

As he reached forward to kiss Tuscus, his arms tight again about him, feeling the bones and muscles stronger than he had known them, the muscles the muscles of a man and not a boy, the eyes not the tearful, trembling ones he had watched for so many days and nights, but the ones of someone who has come out on the other side of shock. Tuscus' skin shifted to match Jen's as Jen bent closer and he held his head back, looking up, and the Jen opened his mouth slightly, and Tuscus did the same, though neither saw the other do so, and their lips met. The clouds rolled in.

The beam dimmed until it was no longer visible. The clouds would trap the heat in as Cain wheeled its way away from the sun, as it had every year, as the Ship dumped energy still but less so, doing the life-preserving job that rightfully earned it the name of god, just enough to keep the clouds in the air. It was enough to warm the planet and let the rains continue, the perpetual rain that broke only at the middle distances of the orbit, the eternal rain that parted only briefly each day, leaving the smell of nothing in the air, the sky purged the rest of the day, the boats and buildings dripping along gutters and gargoyles into the water, the trees fighting as they truly can, routing water to and from each other, alliances already forming in the forests on the flow of the rain through the branches, and the rain poured on.

The rain fell onto Jen and Tuscus sitting together, kissing deeply but tentatively though the drops that beat heavily onto their skin, rolling through their clothes, from Jen's hands where he held Tuscus' head gently, along the littlest finger, around the wrist, rivers on the underside, the arm hair guided into a single path that fell down to the ground at the elbow, the water from Tuscus flowing along his supporting arm, and the rain from each pooled together around them before dripping off of the platform they were sitting on, and they kissed for as long as it rained.

Suggested Reading

These are some of the books that were my source material back when I was first writing this book, from 1993 to 1998. There is much more about ancient Sparta, classical Rome, Venice, the Soviet and Maoist states, and various attempts at utopia, as well as my own travels in Eastern Europe after the Velvet Revolutions, so this list is fundamentally incomplete.

Literature

Asimov, Isaac. *Foundation.* (Books 1-3)
Blake, William. "The Four Zoas"
Herbert, Frank. *Dune.* (Books 1, 2)
Kafka, Franz. *Complete Works.*
McCaffrey, Ann. *Dragonriders of Pern.* (Books 1-3)
More, Thomas. *Utopia.*
Shakespeare, William. "The Tempest"
Simmons, Dan. *Hyperion.* (Books 1, 2)
Zamyatin, Yevgeny. *We.*

Nonfiction

Diamond, Jared. *Guns, Germs, and Steel.*
Gonick, Larry. *Cartoon History of the Universe.* (Books 1-3)
Hsu, Immanuel. *The Rise of Modern China.*
St. John of Damascus. *Apologia Against Those Who Decry Holy Images.*
Liudprand of Cremona. *Embassy to Constantinople.*
Plutarch. *Lives.*
Spence, Jonathan. *The Search for Modern China.*

About the Author

Joseph Cadotte works as an editor, game designer, and general gadfly at an educational software company. He has worked with technological solutions to pedagogical problems since 1993. He has a BA in English from the University of Michigan ('95) and an MFA in Creative Writing from the University of Washington ('98). He longs to return to the oddest place on Earth, Knoxville, TN, with his implausibly hot wife, Cordelia, a gormless dog, and two annoyed cats.

About Old Sins

Frustrated with the way large publishing companies treat their authors, Joseph Cadotte founded Old Sins to be a governed author and illustrator cooperative, focusing on high quality and academically rigorous genre fiction. Our work is targeted to adults, young adults, and advanced juveniles, with the idea that complex themes need exploring through enjoyable and interesting art. Visit us at oldsins.com.

www.ingramcontent.com/pod-product-compliance
Lightning Source LLC
Chambersburg PA
CBHW021006120726
47905CB00009B/2875